FREE AND EASY

FREE AND EASY

Anthony Hontoir

DOWNWOOD BOOKS

Downwood Books
Downwood House, Marlpit Lane, Porthcawl, CF36 5EG

First published in Great Britain by
Downwood Books 2008

Copyright © Anthony Hontoir 2008

ISBN 978-0-9558041-0-6

Set in 12pt. Garamond

Printed and bound in Great Britain by
Mackays of Chatham

AUTHOR'S NOTE
This story is set in Kingshampton Comprehensive School
in the small provincial market town of Kingshampton in
1973-74. All of the characters and events, together
with the town and the school, are entirely fictitious.

Chapter 1

It all began when Miles Randolph made up his mind to do as little in life as possible.

Miles Randolph was tired of being in school because it always used to make him think of work, and he was tired of work. It was only one day after he had started to do nothing seriously that he began to wonder why the idea had not occurred to him before. He was in the second year of the sixth form at Kingshampton Comprehensive School when the thought of examinations could be postponed no longer, and his decision to abandon all work was taken in the knowledge that something needed to be done to make his life more enjoyable. He was happy to remain his usual lazy self and tell other people how he would really prefer to be doing something far worse, such as working very hard, so that the prospect would make him pleased to think how fortunate and wise he was to be avoiding it in the first place.

Miles's school wasn't such a bad place for not doing a great deal of anything. The days always seemed to pass fairly quickly and there was usually enough spare time, in the form of free periods, to prevent him from getting too much work, if it wasn't possible to avoid getting any altogether. The upper school occupied the old classical Georgian-style Kingshampton Grammar School buildings and the lower school was situated in the somewhat plainer edifice of the Secondary Modern nearby, separated from each other by the school playing fields which were used for rugby, soccer and hockey in the autumn and winter terms and cricket in the summer.

If he was lucky he might even find Francesca, the young secretary's secretary, in the office first thing in the morning when he went in to say that he had arrived. The office was a large room with a big desk in the middle, a tall filing cabinet in one corner and two bright lights suspended from the ceiling like miniature globes. It always had a nice fresh smell of perfume about it. Francesca sat behind her own little table next to the window surrounded by boxes of paper and files of various colours and never seemed to do anything except type letters all day. On the floor by her feet were dozens of screwed-up pieces of paper which had rolled off her table or missed the waste-paper basket in the corner.

She was alone in the room when he entered, and he smiled at her in his usual way.

"You're late again, Miles," she said.

"I know," said Miles, "but I'm trying very hard not to be."

She laughed and got up from her chair to go over to the desk where all the registers were piled up one on top of another, took out his form register, marked him in and put it back on top of the pile.

"That's what you always say, isn't it?"

Miles pretended to think of an excuse.

"The bus was late," he said brightly, even though he didn't get the bus.

"Again?"

"Yes."

"I don't know what they'd say if they knew."

"Who's they?" he wondered.

Whenever Francesca was on her own in the office, Miles used to stay talking for a few minutes and keep her from her work, which she never seemed to mind. If she was busier than usual she got him to do the register himself, which was rather trusting of her since he would simply mark himself in for the afternoon as well and go home at lunchtime – although they didn't let him get away with that for long. In fact he had tried nearly everything he could possibly think of to avoid doing too much work.

He fancied Francesca because she was older than he was and he knew that she would be wasting herself on anyone but him. He had asked her out countless times in the past and on each occasion she had politely refused. If she had accepted, he probably wouldn't have fancied her any more, but all this polite refusing just made him fancy her all the more. She was very pretty and had long black hair tied up in a pony-tail with a big gold clasp.

"Working hard?" she asked, knowing perfectly well that he wasn't.

"Of course," he lied shamelessly, knowing perfectly well that she knew he wasn't, and pleased that she had asked him because it meant that she knew he wanted to take her out and was just trying to lead him on.

"Really, Miles," she said disapprovingly. "Everyone here knows it's not true. I don't know how you can say such a thing."

"Who's to say I'm not?" he demanded.

"Who's to say you are?" she countered logically. "I don't know what they'd say if they knew."

"But they don't know," he said in a whisper and put one finger to his lips. "And you won't tell anyone, will you?"

He blew her a kiss, left the office quietly and walked across the empty lobby to the assembly hall, where he opened one of the doors at the back and peeped in. The whole of the upper school was in there, facing the front of the hall for morning assembly. A group of teachers sat up on the stage and somebody was already standing at the lectern, reading out a passage from the bible. When Miles could see that nobody was looking in his direction, he slipped in through the swing doors and pretended that he had been there all the time.

One day he arrived at school quite early for a change, much to the surprise of Francesca, who didn't see him at all that day, and he wandered into the hall at the same time that everyone else in the school was trying to get in. Morning assembly was always a very noisy affair to begin with because all of the forms converged on the hall at the same time and spent a good five minutes pushing and shoving their way through the lobby, jamming themselves in the hall doors before spilling out into the large school hall. Then they would congregate in their own form groups, leaning against the cream and grey walls or sitting on the radiators, talking and shouting to each other in the most disorderly manner imaginable. Miles thought that they were all mad. He stood on his own at the back, watching as everyone continued to pour in from the lobby. Two girls from the sixth form walked past him and his casual gaze, which had wandered around most parts of the room from the floor to the ceiling, from the windows to the stage and from one passing face to another, suddenly found itself following them, looking at one girl in particular. Her name was Suzanne and she was blonde, slim and very pretty. He liked her pale blue eyes and freckled nose. She dressed like all the other girls in a white school shirt and tie, usually hanging loose at the neck, and a short dark grey skirt; and the fashion for wearing tights, socks and high-heeled shoes meant that like most of the other girls she also had a very nice pair of legs on show, although Miles decided that hers were particularly attractive. Soon, she and her friend were lost amidst the growing crowd and before long he had forgotten about her again.

The noise in the hall got so bad on one occasion that nobody could hear when the teachers arrived, and the one with the loudest voice shouted for silence. Since not all of the staff could possibly fit on the stage, they were supposed to attend morning assembly every so often at regular intervals on a rota, but some teachers seemed more adept than others at remaining in the staff room or finding that they had other tasks that took them elsewhere, so it was usually the same group that turned up, including the strict disciplinarians who would not stand for any nonsense. If one or two particular teachers attended, the hall fell into complete silence from the moment they entered. If the headmaster put in one of his rare appearances, nobody even noticed. Assembly consisted of a hymn, a passage from the bible, a prayer and the reading of school notices. Sometimes the small school orchestra occupied the floor at the front of the hall under the supervision of the music teacher, and finished off the proceedings with a rendering of Brahms or Mozart. The presence of the headmaster indicated either that last year's examination results had been very good and he had a few certificates to hand out, or that the school rugby team had won an important match. The school would then have to listen attentively when one of the team, battered and bruised with broken nose and cauliflower ears, mounted the stage to mumble his way through a written account of the victory which hardly anybody could hear because he was too self-conscious to speak up.

"I can't take any more of this," muttered Miles to himself, casting a last look around for Suzanne, and decided not to go to assembly again. He slipped out of the hall and made his way up to the physics laboratory, which was his form room. Nobody would ever think of looking for him there. The door was unlocked so he opened it quietly and went in.

Brian and Dave were already there, sitting on wooden stools at the far end of the lab, playing with some of the experiments. When they heard the door open they both turned in surprise and hurriedly tried to pretend that they weren't doing anything, but once they discovered it was only Miles, they turned around again and carried on with what they were doing while he wandered up to them.

"What are you two doing in here?" he demanded.

"Oh, nothing," said Brian airily, "we're just conducting an experiment, that's all."

Somebody had left a Van de Graaf electrostatic generator on one of the benches from the previous day and Dave was now busily plugging it in to one of the electric wall sockets and switching it on. Slowly it began to make a low whirring sound, then, once its small motor had run up to full speed, it started to perform. All of a sudden there were sharp loud cracking sounds and long vivid blue sparks flashed across the gap between its large highly-polished dome and a small metal ball that stood alongside on the end of a thin rod.

"Good, isn't it?" said Dave, enjoying himself. He turned a knob at the bottom to make it go faster and the sparks came more frequently.

"Well, I think it's all pointless," decided Miles. "I mean, what's the point in it?"

"I don't know," said Dave vaguely. "I don't think there is a point. But it looks good."

"I wonder what would happen," said Brian, "if you touched it?" He tried to imagine somebody touching the metal dome.

"Give it a try," suggested Dave.

Brian placed his hand on the machine and immediately the long wavy hair on his head stuck upwards and outwards. "Most invigorating," he said.

"Turn it off," said Miles nervously.

Dave reluctantly switched it off and the whirring subsided. Miles looked around the laboratory.

"What are you two doing in here anyway?" he asked with a faint trace of suspicion.

Brian looked affronted.

"What do you mean?" he said indignantly. "We always stay up here so we can miss going to assembly."

"You're not supposed to do that!" said Miles, who had no idea that this sort of thing was going on behind his back.

"Why not?"

"It's not allowed."

Dave had a sudden thought. "If that's the case, what are *you* doing in here then?"

"That's got nothing to do with it!" snapped Miles impatiently.

Dave decided to switch on the generator again to continue with his morning's amusement, but at the same moment Brian pulled the plug out from the wall and so nothing

12

happened. "What's gone wrong now?" said Dave. "It's not working." He started to shake it and it began to sway to and fro.

"Be careful," said Brian, and put the plug back in. The thing started to whirr again and Dave let out a cry of anguish. "Ouch! Turn it off!" he yelled. Then he let go of it and ran around the lab, clutching one hand tightly under his other arm.

"I think you've just given him a slight shock," said Miles severely to Brian.

"There was nothing slight about it!" shouted Dave loudly, running past the blackboard. He came around on the other side of them and snatched the plug out again, glaring at Brian.

"Are you all right?" inquired Miles.

"No I'm not!" said Dave, feeling perfectly all right again. "That thing is dangerous!" He made a mental note to keep his hands well away from it in future.

A few moments later voices could be heard outside the lab door and they decided that assembly must be over so it was time to go somewhere else, such as the library. They left their form room, which would soon be occupied for the first lesson of the day, and walked along the wide balcony, which ran almost the entire length of the school, until they reached the library where most of the sixth form went during free periods to carry on with their studies.

The library was a long rectangular room divided up into three parts by two dividing walls. It was situated directly above the lobby, the office and the headmaster's study. The bookshelves that lined its walls were filled with books on all subjects imaginable, and it was a peaceful haven for all of those who wished to carry on with their work. Anyone in the school could borrow books from the library, but only at certain times of the day such as breaktime or during the lunch hour. It was run by the librarian, a prim-faced bespectacled middle-aged woman who was assisted by a small team of boys and girls who were taught by one of the

English masters and who seemed to be the favoured few. They were invariably condescending in manner and had high opinions of themselves, carrying out their book-lending duties with the attitude of a glittering elite given the tiresome and hopeless job of dealing with a bunch of useless and ignorant peasants.

Miles spent most of his time in the library reading detective novels which he found on one of the shelves once by accident. Well at least it was better than Brian, because all he did was sit there with a chemistry textbook open in front of him at the chapter on distillation. One day Miles had an idea and when Brian wasn't looking he turned the book upside down and Brian continued flicking the pages over quite happily at regular intervals without noticing. Dave devoted his time to sitting by the window with his head down on his folded arms, apparently fast asleep. This, he once explained, was because the pressures of life were too great for him to survive in any other posture, a situation brought about by a nasty hangover from the night before.

Everyone else in the library got on with their work and regarded Miles, Brian and Dave as idle layabouts. If anything disturbed the peace and calm, a door would open and out would pop the librarian like a troll from her small room at the back and remonstrate with the wrongdoer. Sometimes the deputy headmaster would pay a visit to the library, often for the purpose of going mysteriously into the tiny storeroom that stood next to the librarian's little office. Most people suspected that he kept bottles of gin hidden in there, which shows how malicious rumours can easily get out of hand; and yet nobody knew the reason for his frequent visits.

At Miles's table they always had to be careful in case any of their teachers entered the room to find out why they weren't attending their lessons.

"Why do you reckon we're still in school at all?" asked Brian, wondering whether Miles or Dave might know the answer.

Miles sat back and scratched his head thoughtfully. Dave

apparently remained asleep.

"Because they haven't thrown us out yet," said Miles brightly.

"That is true," agreed Brian, and turned to look at Dave. "Why is he sleeping all the time?"

"Because he's tired," explained Miles. "Dave is one of these people who are permanently tired."

Dave shot up immediately as if he had been sitting on a powerful spring. "No I am not!" he protested. "I'm just recovering from a very bad electric shock. What I've got to put up with when you two are around is nobody's business."

"It's too bad," sympathised Miles.

"Yes, much too bad," said Brian.

"What's too bad?" demanded Dave suspiciously.

"What you've got to put up with when the two of us are around," said Miles. "We feel very sorry for you. Now go back to sleep."

Miles usually stayed in the library for the rest of the morning, although sometimes he went to a physics or chemistry practical lesson when he felt like it, which would only be once a week, and after a while he got a bit fed up with that, too. Brian and Dave went regularly to their practical lessons because they used to play around with everything and do nothing. Miles gazed around the library and wondered how everyone else could be so absorbed in their work. What were they hoping to achieve? Most mornings the room was full from the moment assembly finished and remained so until after the first bell had gone. From then on, people seemed to drift in and out all the time.

Miles looked at a group of girls sitting at a table on the other side of the room. They were first year sixth-formers. He kept his eye on them and soon afterwards the library door opened and two other girls came in and joined their table. One of the newcomers was the girl called Suzanne. He watched her with growing interest. Brian was looking at her as well, and he grinned at Miles.

"Not bad," he said.

"Not bad at all. Do you know her?"

"No," said Brian, "but Dave probably does." He turned to Dave and woke him up. "See that girl over there? The one with blonde hair. What's her name?"

"It's not her name I want to find out, I already know it," said Miles. "She's called Suzanne. I just want to find out more about *her*."

"She's a very nice girl," said Dave sleepily through bleary eyes. "But that's only my humble opinion. She might well be horrible."

"Oh no," said Miles, "I think she's very nice indeed." His voice trailed to nothing but he kept his eyes intently on her. Suddenly and quite deliberately she lifted her head and looked across the room at him. He turned away in an instant, as if his mind were occupied with other thoughts, and when he glanced back a few moments later it was the girl's turn to look away, but the exchange was enough for Miles. Hers was only a short visit, for soon she stood up with her bag on one arm, spoke some parting words to her friends and walked across to the door, slowly and rhythmically. "She knows I'm watching her," thought Miles, aware that his heart was beating faster, and when she opened the door to leave the library, their eyes met again. He sat back in his seat and a smile spread slowly across his face.

Chapter 2

The effort of each morning was so tiring that Miles and Brian had to go along to the sixth form common room at lunchtime, where they collapsed into comfortable low metal-framed seats with black plastic cushions to eat their sandwiches while Dave went down to the school canteen for a cooked dinner.

The sixth form common room was crowded all day with people who sought refuge from their lessons to play cards, smoke cigarettes and drink coffee, but, unlike Miles, Brian and Dave, they were people who attended their classes regularly and got on with their work. They were only idle layabouts in their spare time. Some of them were not even idle layabouts at all. Nobody stayed in the common room for long, but everyone who went in there knew the risk of being found out, for most of their pastimes involved doing something that was forbidden in the school rules.

Accordingly, someone always had to keep a careful watch to make sure none of the staff ever surprised them by entering the room unexpectedly. Occasionally the deputy headmaster would creep up quietly to the door and pounce swiftly on them, and the sheer horror on his face upon entering such a terrible den of iniquity was often worth being there just to see. He would never confiscate a complete pack of cards – only half a dozen or so, leaving the rest where they were to show how infuriating he could be. The card players occupied a far corner of the room, out of sight from the door, but the deputy still found them.

The common room had a coffee machine, but it never seemed to work properly. Instead of coffee it gave tea, and instead of tea it gave hot chocolate, sometimes with sugar and sometimes without. Sometimes it gave nothing but kept the money, other times it rejected the money and poured out a stream of cold water. The prefects complained to the office about it but nothing was ever done. It was one of the school's curiosities.

Since Miles and Brian only used the common room as a convenient place to have lunch, once they had finished they went down to the canteen and waited for Dave to emerge, often clutching a handful of second-helping chocolate sponge pudding or apple tart. Lunchtime put them on equal terms with the rest of the school, including the teachers, because this was the one hour in the school day when nobody did anything and they felt conspicuously the same. They could walk around the school, or wander across the playing fields, they could join in the informal games of football in the big yard at the back, but nothing appealed as much as taking a stroll into town, a small privilege granted to the oldest pupils.

Whoever made the rules did not envisage that the right to walk into town included an entitlement to visit the local public houses, and it is possible that none of the teachers who availed themselves of the opportunity for a lunchtime drink ever imagined that their pupils would think of doing the same.

"What was dinner like today?" asked Miles when they met up with Dave outside the canteen, and Dave pulled a face.

"Same as usual," observed Brian.

"Awful muck," grumbled Dave. "I don't know why I keep eating it."

"Why *do* you keep eating it?" asked Miles out of interest.

"Because my mother keeps giving me the money to buy it," explained Dave, "and I'm too honest to cheat her."

Every morning Miles used to ask his father if he would buy

him a little car so that he could drive himself to school in it and take his friends out during the lunch hour for a race into town, and every morning the answer was no.

"What did your old man say this morning about buying you a car?" asked Brian curiously as they walked through the empty lobby.

"He said no," said Miles, who was waiting for the day to come when his father would be away on business so that he could borrow his car and bring it to school without anyone at home knowing.

"What I could do with," announced Dave suddenly while they were meandering slowly around one of the deserted quadrangles, "is a drink."

"When do you think your old man will be away, so you can borrow *his* car and bring it in?" asked Brian.

"I don't know. I keep asking him but he never says," said Miles. "If I ask him too often, he'll begin to suspect something."

"God, I was drunk last night," said Dave even more suddenly. Every night at about nine o' clock Dave went down to the pub and had a few beers for an hour or two before going back home again for supper – although nobody believed him. "You don't believe me, do you?"

Miles looked at him.

"Don't believe you what?"

"You don't believe I was drunk last night."

"How would I know if you were drunk last night? Well, were you?"

"Yes."

"You're right – I don't believe you."

"Not a bit?"

"No."

"Not even a *little* bit?"

Miles shook his head and Dave began to dance about with frustration. "Why not?" he demanded.

"If you really want to know what I think," said Miles, "I don't think you've ever been drunk in your entire life."

"Right!" said Dave quickly. "I'll prove it to you."

"Perhaps we'll take your word for it," said Brian generously, who had heard about some of Dave's drinking sessions before and didn't know what to make of them.

Most lunchtimes they set off from school to walk into Kingshampton. It was one of those small market towns that had grown, like so many other places, into something altogether larger, with industrial estates on its outskirts. The town centre was still old and rather quaint and narrow, with a medieval quarter at its heart where the upper storeys of the buildings overhung the pavements, a fourteenth-century stone bridge crossed the river and a Norman church stood on a ridge of higher ground.

By the time they had left the school and arrived in the middle of town, Dave was insisting on going into every pub they came across. Soon afterwards they lost him altogether. One moment he was walking beside them, then before they knew what was happening he had disappeared and was nowhere to be seen.

"Where's Dave?" said Miles, noticing his absence, and they stopped to look around.

"I'll give you one guess," said Brian after a brief search of the street revealed no sign of him. "He's gone into the *Crown and Anchor.*"

Miles smacked a hand across his eyes. "Oh hell, the idiot! We'd better go and get him out, before someone catches him. Listen, I think I've got an idea."

"I'm listening," said Brian receptively. "I'm in the mood for a good laugh."

Sure enough, Dave was in the *Crown and Anchor.* They had been passing it when he spotted two girls from the nearby technical college going in through the door of the public bar. At the sight of him looking at them, the girls turned to give him a sideways glance and giggled to each other. Without saying a word to Miles or Brian, Dave ran back quickly and followed them in. It was a small public house with a dark, cosy atmosphere and most of the other young people in there were from the college, with not a familiar school face among them. Dave thought that the crowded bar looked safe enough to chance a quick one.

Miles and Brian entered in time to see him take his first sip from a pint of beer.

"Oh, hello," he said. "I thought you'd both gone. Have you decided to come in for a drink too?"

"No," said Miles severely, "we've come in to get you out. Do you realise what they'd say if we were caught in here?"

"No," said Dave, looking interested, "but I shouldn't think they'd say anything much. In any case, I've never been caught yet."

"That's not the point."

"Well, what *would* happen, in your opinion?"

"They'd probably have you suspended."

"What – from the school?"

"No, from the neck. What do you think? And us too, if they find all three of us in here."

Dave thought about it for a while, still sipping his beer. "Do you really think they would?" he said in alarm and fascination.

"Bound to," said Brian cheerfully. "It could be the answer to a prayer."

Dave looked down at the glass in his hand and its incriminating contents.

"Well, hang on a minute, will you? I've got all this to get through first. I won't be a couple of seconds."

Brian began to look intrigued. "Are you going to drink all that down in one go?" he inquired, wondering what would happen if Dave did.

Dave smiled confidently at him and prepared to start tipping the glass back.

"Oh yes, of course," he said. "It's what you might call an acquired technique. There aren't many people who can do it, you know."

"He's going to make a fool of himself now," groaned Miles and got ready to close his eyes.

"It's taken months of practice," said Dave, ignoring him.

"Come on then, get on with it and let's get out of here."

"All right, all right," said Dave. "I've got to get myself ready, you can't rush this sort of thing."

"You said it was only going to take a couple of seconds."

"That's once I get started. It can take ages to get prepared. It's all to do with controlling your breathing, I think."

Miles began to walk around in circles.

"Will you get on with it!" he hissed.

Several customers standing nearby had broken off their own conversation and were watching in fascination, as though they were all expecting Dave to topple over backwards at the end of it and fall flat on the floor. With great concentration he raised the glass to his lips and winked broadly at Miles and Brian.

"Well, here goes," he said. "Cheers!"

"Cheers," said Miles and Brian together.

At that moment they heard the bar door open and Brian grabbed Miles by the arm. "Look out!" he said in a hoarse whisper.

Dave choked over his beer, got some of the froth in his face and slammed the glass down again. "What's the matter?" he asked in a frightened voice.

Miles and Brian caught hold of him and dragged him around the side of the bar out of sight.

"Did you see who just came in?" moaned Brian.

"Of course I did," replied Miles dramatically. "That's done it now."

"I didn't see who it was. What's happening?" asked Dave plaintively, his voice rising higher, wondering with an awful feeling of dread what it would be like to be suspended and how his parents would take the news.

"I think it's all right," whispered Brian, peering around the bar. "He hasn't seen us yet."

Dave frantically tried to find a place to hide his glass, which was still somehow attached firmly to his hand. *"Who* hasn't seen us yet?" he screeched.

"What do you mean, he hasn't seen us?" demanded Miles, paying no attention to Dave who was hopping about in agitation. "He must have seen us! Dave was standing right in the middle of the room. Do you think there's a back way out of this place?"

They started to search for another door and then Dave's eyes fell on a flowerpot standing on the window-sill with a large rubber plant in it with enormous green leaves. In desperation he rushed up to it and emptied the contents of his glass into the pot.

The barmaid saw him and she shrieked in amazement: "Hey, what do you think you're doing to my plant?"

"Our friend was just watering it," said Miles soothingly. "He thought it was looking a bit limp."

"But he'll kill it with that!"

"Well if that's the case, madam, we're certainly not coming here again. Good day to you."

Brian beckoned to them. "I think he's gone again. Come on, let's get out of here quickly."

"Who is it?" asked Dave persistently.

"Never mind that now," said Miles, "we'll tell you later. Go on."

They moved forward cautiously and edged their way around the tables as quietly as they could and then they made for the door in a sudden rush and left the bar. The door banged shut behind them and they stopped breathlessly in the street to look at each other.

"That was close!" grinned Brian.

"Next time we'd better go somewhere else," said Dave shakily, but then Miles and Brian began to laugh. He stared at them. "What's the matter with you two?"

"Oh, nothing," said Miles.

Dave discovered that he was still holding the beer glass in his hand. Miles and Brian shook their heads reproachfully at him and smirked at each other.

"You certainly can't take it back now," said Miles at last.

"But I can't carry it around with me for the rest of the

afternoon!" moaned Dave.

"It looks as if you'll have to," said Brian.

"But someone might see me. I can't walk back into school with it, can I?"

"You'd better try and lose it then, hadn't you?" advised Miles. "Leave it on a wall, or stick it in a hedge. Do something with it quickly, though."

They started to make their way back to school. By the time they got there, Dave was still holding the glass. Every time he had come across a low wall or a hedge there was always someone passing by who would see him.

"It looks as though you'll just have to take it in with you, doesn't it?" said Brian.

"Oh hell!"

"There's still a bit left in the bottom, too," pointed out Miles. "I wouldn't let them see that if I were you, or they might think you've been drinking." He and Brian started to laugh again.

"It's all very well for you both to make a joke of it," said Dave ruefully, "but what happens if I'm caught with this in my hand?"

"Oh, for heaven's sake give it to me," said Miles and took the glass from him. With a quick glance around to make sure nobody was watching, he drained it and gave it back to Dave. "Mmmm, not bad."

"Who came into the pub?" asked Dave again.

"Nobody," said Miles.

Dave stared at him blankly for a moment.

"What do you mean?" There was a trace of dawning awareness in his voice.

"There wasn't anyone there," said Brian.

"There wasn't anyone there!" shouted Dave. "But I heard the door open."

"That was somebody leaving."

"*What?*" yelled Dave.

"It was somebody going out," said Miles slowly and patiently in the tone that might be used to explain something to a dimwit.

"Do you mean you made all that up about someone from the school coming in?"

They nodded.

Dave exploded in a long tirade of spluttered insults, words that could not possibly by repeated without causing offence to certain readers.

"I thought it was rather amusing myself," said Miles, and jumped out of the way when Dave aimed his fist at him.

"So I wasted all that beer for nothing?"

They nodded again. "All over the plant, too. Such a shame."

"Do you mean you stopped me just as I was about to start *drinking* it – and there was *nobody there at all?*"

They kept on nodding.

"I can't think of the words to describe you!"

"How about kind and considerate?" suggested Miles. "We did it for your own good."

When they got back inside the school, Dave kept the glass furtively hidden under his blazer. The first person they saw wandering aimlessly about in the lobby was Peter, who was in the same year as themselves but was studying art. He spent most of his time in the art room, working on his latest hideous creation or arranging the next school dance. All of his ideas were to do with changing perspective and he thought he was quite brilliant. He went in search of perfection and knew that one day he would find it. His ideas, those concepts that he held in his mind, were always so *elusive;* one minute they were there, filling his imagination with clear and exciting thoughts, and the next minute they had gone again as though they had never existed, but he knew that he would succeed. Most people thought that Peter was slightly mad, with his long hair and enormous round spectacles, but this did not bother him because he thought that all of those people who thought he was mad were mad themselves.

Miles certainly thought he was crazy and treated him as a

very close friend whose craziness might rub off on him, thus making Miles crazy himself – which he was anyway.

"Hello, Peter," he said. "How art thou?"

"My art is fine," replied Peter, and looked curiously at Dave. "Why are you hiding a beer glass under your jacket, Dave?"

"It's a long story," said Miles hastily, "and one which we will tell you one day when we have the time, but the point is, Peter, we brought it back for you."

"For me?" said Peter in surprise.

"Yes," said Miles generously. "It must have been something you said to us the other day about your latest piece of art – you know, your special project or whatever you call it – and we thought that the inclusion of a beer glass might add something to it." Miles leaned forward and nodded encouragingly. "Don't you think?"

"Well, er, *yes*, I see exactly what you mean," said Peter, taking the glass that Dave had thrust into his hands and examining it carefully.

"There must be a statement in it somewhere," said Brian, making a gesture with his hands.

"Oh, there is!" agreed Peter. "Most definitely! I don't really know how to thank you enough for thinking of it. It's just what I wanted."

"Well, that's excellent," said Miles, smiling warmly. "It means it was all worthwhile." He drew Peter aside and lowered his voice. "I wouldn't stand there holding it for everyone to see, though, Peter. If I were you I'd take it straight down to the art room."

"Of course," said Peter. "Thank you, boys." He turned to walk away with it and they set off quickly in the opposite direction. After a few moments, when they had gone, he returned to the lobby and put the glass down with exquisite care on a chair outside the headmaster's study, moving it firstly one way and then the other until he was satisfied with its position. "My first exhibition," he said to himself, full of satisfaction.

Chapter 3

Miles had never come across anyone like Brian before. Brian was a muddle of contradictions, a living conundrum. He was friendly, distant, calm, excitable, clever and incapable; sometimes shy, occasionally diffident, rarely troubled by overwork and never completely persuaded by anything. He had few aims other than to pass through school with the least possible effort and, to his credit, he was doing a magnificent job.

Brian could twist anything to his advantage except girls, and the fact that he could twist anything to his advantage belied the fact that he was hopelessly unable to ask girls to go out with him, which he desperately wanted them to because he fancied them so much. Most girls seemed to laugh at him because he had long curly hair and a nose which turned up, whereas they weren't really laughing at him at all because he stood over six feet tall and commanded the sort of respect which only the prefects had and didn't deserve, and Brian wasn't even a prefect. Neither was Miles, who felt he ought to be. Nobody was sure whether or not Dave was a prefect because he never wore a prefect's badge but always got himself picked out in assembly to take the long pole from the corner of the hall and open the windows, which he casually passed on to someone in the fourth form who suspected that it was best not to argue.

Each of them regarded the library as a kind of sanctum sanctorum from where they could escape all the madness and absurdity of the classroom which only the library was capable of mollifying. Miles had given up hope that others might follow his example of idleness, thereby strengthening his argument that work was implacably futile. They were all too occupied with their own petty ideologies of survival to realise that he was the only one who possessed any degree of sense.

"One day all this is going to end," predicted Miles. "One day somebody's going to wake up to the fact that we know too much for our own good and need to start unlearning what we already know, if it's not too late."

"You're off your head," said Nigel, who sometimes lent his chemistry notes to Brian when Brian forgot to bring his chemistry textbook, which Miles only turned upside-down to prove that Brian never read a word of it. "As if that could ever happen."

"And nobody bothers to make constructive replies any more," complained Miles witheringly. "Think about what I'm saying and you might understand."

"When I'm a success," said Nigel, "you're going to be a failure."

"In whose opinion?" asked Miles.

"Anyone who's got any sense."

"Define sense."

"What?"

"I said define sense, if you can."

Nigel paused and bit his lip, frowning. Then he snapped his fingers together. "The power to understand a sensation," he proposed confidently. "To interpret or comprehend an outward experience by examining it with a precise, balanced mind."

"Define balance," said Miles.

"Equilibrium, which is a state where opposed forces cancel each other out," said Nigel.

"Define force," said Miles.

"Any cause which changes the speed or direction of a particle of matter," said Nigel, who had obviously been studying his definitions.

Arnold was listening on the other side of the table. "You're the matter," he said condescendingly. "What do you know about anything?"

Miles disliked Arnold, who was a self-satisfied little swot.

"I know a lot more than you think," said Miles serenely.

"I don't think much about what you know," sneered Arnold, and got on with his own reading.

"Why do they call you Arnold, Arnold?" asked Miles suddenly.

"Because it's my name," replied Arnold. "Stupid."

One day they marched Miles off to see the deputy and explain to him why he always talked in the library instead of working as he should have been doing.

"*I* don't talk in the library," said the deputy indignantly. "In fact I hardly ever go in the library."

They shook their heads solemnly and pointed to Miles.

"Oh," said the deputy, and waved them away.

Miles looked around in surprise.

"Who are they, sir?" he asked.

"They're prefects," said the deputy. "I've asked them to stop people talking in the library. Why were you talking in the library when it's forbidden?"

"I wasn't, sir," said Miles.

"Are you calling me a liar?" demanded the deputy.

"No sir, I'm not calling you a liar."

"What are you doing, then?"

"I'm not calling you *anything*, sir."

"Then tell me why you were talking in the library when you know it's forbidden."

"I wasn't talking in the library, sir."

"So you are calling me a liar!" shouted the deputy. "If you weren't talking, what *were* you doing?"

"I was discussing, sir," explained Miles.

"What were you discussing?" asked the deputy with great suspicion.

"I was discussing work, sir."

"Work? What kind of work?"

"The kind of work that's necessary to get on, sir," said Miles knowingly.

"I see," mused the deputy slowly. "Yes, I see."

So Miles got the deputy's special permission to sit in the library all day and discuss the kind of work that was necessary for him to get on, but he was not allowed to talk. He could ruminate and argue, make suggestions and postulate but he still wasn't allowed to *talk*. He thanked the deputy and made his way back up to the library, where he spent the rest of his time ruminating and arguing, making suggestions and postulating, but he never *talked* any more because it was forbidden and the prefects were there to make sure everybody obeyed the rules except themselves.

Miles decided that he wouldn't have minded being a prefect himself. After all, there were so many things he could confiscate. There were gob-stoppers, catapults, bubble-gum, water pistols, transistor radios, make-up, perfume – the list seemed endless. Of course, all objects of confiscation were meant to be properly shared out amongst the confiscators, but mostly they went straight into their own pockets or bags.

Miles enjoyed bluffing about the amount of work he did because he found that people believed him. Even Brian and Dave found themselves believing in him. He was a very believable individual. Dave believed that one day Miles would borrow his old man's car and bring it to school so that they could race down to town in it at lunchtime. Dave's mother owned a Mini, and he decided that one day *he* would borrow it and bring it to school just to make Miles envious. Dave's trouble was that he couldn't drive because he spent most of his spare time with Jane, the girl whom nobody knew anything about, except for when he was drinking in his local pub which all of his friends refused to believe.

Brian's trouble was that he fell desperately in love with every girl who could throw off her school uniform to become a fine young woman. There were plenty of girls who wanted to throw off their school uniforms to become fine young women and were only too anxious to prove themselves with boys, but never with Brian. He found it most disconcerting.

"I wonder what it's like to make love," wondered Brian one day when he got fed up with goggling at all of the most beautiful girls in the sixth form who merely returned his lustful gaze with looks of complete and utter disdain.

"Don't you know?" asked Miles in surprise.

"No," confessed Brian sadly, "I don't know. If I did know, I suppose I wouldn't spend all my time wondering. I always spend my time wondering about things I don't know."

"I don't take maths any more," said Dave tantalisingly. "Aren't I lucky?"

"Is that because you wanted to be a pilot until you found you were frightened of flying?" said Miles unkindly.

Dave's face crumpled up in tremulous, quivering pain. "Don't say things like that," he begged. "Please don't."

Miles grinned.

"Sorry," he said, "but I thought you were pleased not to be taking maths."

"I am," said Dave, "but the reason upsets me."

"Because you wanted to be a pilot?" said Miles.

"Please don't!" said Dave in anguish. "It upsets me to think about it."

"Sorry."

"You don't need to say sorry," said Dave generously. "But thank you for saying it because it makes me feel better."

"What makes you feel better?" asked Miles curiously.

"Not taking maths any more," said Dave. "It makes me feel so much better."

Miles was genuinely puzzled. "But I thought you wanted to be a pilot?"

Dave smacked both hands over his eyes.

"Don't mention that word again," he pleaded.

"What word?"

"The word you just mentioned."

"You mean pilot?"

"No! No! Yes! Oh, *don't!*"

"Touchy, isn't he?" said Miles, turning to Brian.

"One of the touchiest," grumbled Brian, who had his own problems to deal with.

"Dave," said Miles sternly, "calm down."

Dave sprang up and went running around the library, thumping one hand against his head in frustration.

"It's my life you're talking about," he screamed, "and all you can do is tell me to calm down. What else can I do?"

"Give up work altogether," advised Miles. "It's not doing you a bit of good. Take a look at everyone in this room – they're all completely mad."

"Are they?" he asked in a hushed, awe-struck voice. "Really? Are they *all* mad?"

"Well, what do you think?" said Miles with calculated simplicity.

"Oh, I don't know!" said Dave in despair, and he plunged out of the library, slamming the door shut. Miles didn't see a sign of him for at least a week, when he came back to school without any books in his briefcase and only went into the office to pay his dinner money.

Later that day a boy called Philip Rosser walked into the library and went straight over to Miles's table.

"Why aren't you in applied maths?" he demanded.

Miles looked up in surprise. "Because I'm here instead," he replied with disarming logic. "Why?"

"Mr Lester wants to know."

"Why should Mr Lester want to know? I hardly ever go to his lessons. He probably doesn't even know I'm in his class."

Rosser stood at the table, full of self-importance. "Mr Lester happened to ask if anyone knew where you were because he said he hasn't seen you for some time, and Smith said you were in the library. So I said I'd come along and tell you. Are you coming?"

"No thank you," said Miles. "I think I'll give it a miss for another day."

"But I've just walked all the way over from the new building for this!"

"That was very kind of you."

"What am I supposed to tell Mr Lester?" asked Rosser.

"Tell him whatever you like," said Miles with a vaguely disinterested shrug. "Tell him I hate maths, tell him I think he's a rotten teacher, tell him I'd rather be sitting in the library reading a book, as long as it's not a maths book. Really, Rosser, I couldn't give a damn what you tell him, but knowing you for the two-faced crawling little creep that you are, you'll probably just say you couldn't find me. But you can tell your friend Smith that his days here are numbered, because when I get my hands on him…do you get my meaning?"

Rosser turned and left the library with a sneer.

Miles sat back in his chair, scowling. Brian glanced at him.

"Not so good."

"Not so good for that bastard Smith," said Miles darkly. "But I suppose this means I'll have to go next time."

Smith was one of those short, round-faced, bespectacled, smug and detestable people who had been around ever since Miles could remember. He had a squashed-in face with little piggy eyes which made Miles like him even less, and a way of speaking which left little doubt that he had a very high opinion of himself. They had taken a mutual dislike to one another on their first day in form one, and nobody else could stand the sight of Smith either from the moment he first appeared, which was now a long time ago – nobody, that is, except Rosser, who was a friend of his.

Miles started plotting a suitable revenge until Suzanne appeared in the library for the afternoon and then he began doing some plotting of a different kind, wondering how he could get to know her. The thought kept him busy for the rest of the day.

Chapter 4

The headmaster was feeling a bit unhappy about the way things were going. It seemed to him that nobody was taking him seriously and now, when his life should have been running nice and smoothly – well, it wasn't. Instead, what did he have? He had an enormous staff that always seemed to be going absent at the slightest excuse, and then there was his deputy who could only be described as a tiresome nuisance who never seemed capable of running the school, and Lord knows how many other things that he hadn't had time to think about. The headmaster was feeling a very frustrated man.

"What I need," he said one day to the secretary, "is a break. I need a nice long hard break."

"Why do you want a hard break?" asked the secretary.

"I should have thought it was perfectly obvious," he said irritably. "So that I can come back afterwards and enjoy a bit of relaxation."

With a sudden desperate gesture, he began to look at his diary to see what was supposed to be happening. Why was it that people were always ringing up the school and asking to see *him*? What had he done to deserve all the moanings and groanings that were continuously pouring in week after week about so-and-so not being able to do this, or so-and-so getting too much of that?

"Really," he said bitterly, "it's enough to give me a nervous breakdown. I'm sure I'm going to have a nervous breakdown if I carry on like this – in fact, I think I'm having one already. Why can't the deputy deal with it?"

"I think a doctor might be better," advised the secretary helpfully.

"With the work!" He clapped one hand over his brow. "Why can't the deputy deal with all the work – not me, not *me!* He's only got to fob them off with some of the nonsense he was always churning out to that history class of his."

The secretary looked a little uncomfortable.

"Well," she said, "he says it's not his job to be doing that, and anyway he's got enough to do as it is."

Ever since he had been made headmaster, that was all he had been hearing. "What do you mean, it's not his job to be doing that?" he demanded scornfully. "As far as I'm concerned, it's his job to be doing *everything*. Perhaps I can have a bit of peace and quiet then." He couldn't have everyone else in the school running around doing what they wanted, telling him what they were or were not prepared to do just because it suited them. It would have to suit him first and that was the way it was going to be whether they liked it or not.

"It's got to stop," said the headmaster, trying to sound firm and decisive. "From now on, I'm going to make absolutely sure this school is run properly. We must stop all this dodging that's been going on. Dodging work and dodging responsibility. And look at all the litter they're leaving everywhere. I think it's disgusting. And above all, we must keep the rugby team together." He had to admit that if there was one thing he liked it was a good game of rugby. "We're not going to have any more of this nonsense," he went on. "I'm going to get the deputy to give the school a lecture on it."

"On what?" asked the secretary.

He reached into his desk and produced the beer glass.

"Do you know where I found this?" he said. "It was outside my door! I mean, what are they going to do next? Can you answer me that? What *are* they going to do next?"

35

Ever since he had become headmaster, undesirable behaviour was a characteristic of everyday life and he did not like it. The two grass quadrangles, one on either side of the assembly hall, had changed into octangles from where the entire school population, excluding himself, seemed to run all over the corners at some time or another. The gardener had planted flowers there once, and very nice they had looked for a day or two until somebody pulled them up during one of Peter's famous school dances and scattered the petals all around the lobby like confetti. They were still there the following morning and the deputy had given the school a stiff talking-to in assembly that day, but it made no difference. The main trouble was that the headmaster was always too busy to do anything.

"I've got a lot of work to do," he told the secretary, shutting himself inside his study. "I cannot be expected to keep taking assembly every morning."

So he gave up taking assembly every morning and took it once a week instead. Before long it was once a month. He was perfectly happy to stay all morning in his study until it was time to go home for dinner.

He was a short man of a somewhat portly stature who always dressed in the same rather shabby suit of clothes and cracked brown leather shoes; his bald head with its fringe of white hair made him look an old man and his face bore a perpetual faint look of surprise, as if he were still wondering how on earth he had managed to stay there for so long as headmaster. There were many people in the school who wondered the same thing. On more than one occasion he had been mistaken for a tramp by visiting parents whom he was in the process of trying to avoid seeing.

His study was a large pleasant room with a big fireplace opposite his desk. It always made him wince to look at the wall above the fireplace where his predecessor had carefully hung up two of his best canes like crossed swords, and every time he saw them he tried to remember to take them down and snap them in half, but he never did. He simply looked at them and tried to remember to take them down and snap them in half when he wasn't so busy, which would never arise because he always was. The rest of the room was taken up with bookshelves filled with books that he never read, and sitting on his desk in one corner was a grotesque little figure with an ugly face which was meant to be a brass paperweight and which stared at him day after day and made him feel nervous.

"One day I'm going to get rid of that horrible little thing," he told himself every day, and then he had a better idea: he turned it around so that it faced the other way. His visitors noticed it when they came into the study and it always seemed able to hold their attention better than he could.

He managed to get rid of the secretary, who was another one forever pestering him with useless trivial matters, and got up to go into the office next door where he found Miles calmly talking to Francesca the secretary's secretary.

The headmaster stared at him in indignation and looked at the time.

"Are you late, boy?" he demanded.

Miles looked at the time displayed by a clock on the wall.

"Yes, sir." Of course he was late.

"Why?"

"Why?" repeated Miles, thinking.

"Yes, why?"

"Oh, the bus was late, sir."

"What bus?"

"The bus I catch that brings me to school, sir." It was the bus that Miles never caught but always said he did.

"Couldn't you have walked instead?"

"I'd be even later then, sir."

"Well why can't you leave in plenty of time to walk?"

Miles considered the question.

"If I did that, sir, I'd be too early then, because I'd still catch a bus."

The headmaster gaped at him and his face rapidly changed colour.

"Are you trying to be insolent with me?" he demanded furiously.

"No sir, I'm not trying."

"You *are* being insolent with me!"

"Yes sir, I am being insolent with you. I'm terribly sorry, sir."

The headmaster gobbled and Francesca tittered.

"Who *are* you?" he shouted.

"Miles Randolph, sir."

"Randolph?" He frowned. "Do I know that name? Have I heard of you before?" He glared at Francesca, who was trying to pretend she wasn't there. "Do I know this boy?"

"I don't know," she said, fussing about with the registers.

"I'm not in the rugby team, sir," offered Miles helpfully.

The headmaster didn't know him, then. He picked up Miles's register to peruse it in the hope that he might find a string of unexplained absences against the name Randolph, but because of the sweetness and generosity of the secretary's secretary in giving Miles his attendance mark, he was due to be disappointed.

"Make sure you're early next time," he mumbled and went back into his study.

Miles grinned at Francesca.

"Thanks," he said gratefully.

"I really don't know what they'd say if they knew you were late every day, Miles," she said.

"No, nor do I," said Miles, still wondering who *they* were. "But I think I can guess. What are you doing tonight?"

"Miles," she said, "I've told you before."

Miles chuckled happily to himself and wandered out. He bumped into Paul Brown who was loafing about in the lobby. Paul Brown was the captain of the school rugby team. He was huge and enormously stupid, with a great big round face that always looked completely vacant. They made him a prefect as soon as they could so that when he wasn't sorting people out on the rugby field he was sorting them out elsewhere. It was easy because he had a nervous twitch, and this was quite sufficient to break down anyone he confronted into terrified submission. Even some of the staff were a bit frightened of him because they were never sure what he was going to do next. He was a very unpredictable person. Sometimes he twitched for fun, to see the effect it had, but mostly it came of its own accord. When it was his turn to read the lesson from the bible in morning assembly, he twitched all the way through it and the school rolled about the hall in uncontrollable laughter.

One of his best friends was Miles, who happened to be one of the few people in the school who were immune to his peculiar behaviour. When Miles came across him in the lobby, he was busy practising his passing technique and doing a dummy on an invisible opponent with his favourite rugby ball, and he crashed heavily into Miles who went flying back into the office with the ball in his arms. He landed on the desk with a loud *"Oooof!"* and startled Francesca who was about to make a start on her typing.

"Oh, sorry," said Paul, sticking his head around the office door and grinning at them. "It slipped."

"Would it be any good asking what you were doing?" inquired Miles despairingly, picking himself up off the desk.

The headmaster's voice could be heard again, floating out from the study.

"Can I hear that boy Randolph again?" he said sharply.

"Yes, sir," called Miles, "it's me again."

"Oh."

"Did you want to see me, sir?" he sang out wickedly.

"No!"

Miles turned his attention back to Paul. Paul beamed at him.

"What's the matter with you?" said Miles.

"You asked me something," Paul reminded him.

"Did I?"

"Yes. You asked me what I was doing."

"So I did. All right, what the hell *were* you doing?"

"I was practising a dummy on someone," explained Paul

proudly, and turned his grin entirely onto Francesca, whom he fancied. "Good, wasn't it?"

She stared at him in terror, afraid that he was going to take a leap at her.

"Oh, brilliant," said Miles. "Have you noticed that there's a big field outside?"

"Yes," said Paul, "I'm playing out there later. Are you going to wish me good luck?"

"I doubt if you need it," sighed Miles and gave the ball back to him.

"Thanks, Miles," said Paul. "See you around."

Chapter 5

Miles got to school one morning and walked into the library to find he was so early for once that he had the room to himself – almost. In the far corner, over by the door of the storeroom that was always kept locked and never opened by anyone other than the deputy, sat Arnold, who was young enough to look as though he shouldn't be in the sixth form and wise enough to pretend that he wasn't. Arnold wore metal-framed spectacles and had long fair wavy hair that stuck out from his head and often got him into trouble. Arnold was undoubtedly very clever.

"What are you doing?" asked Miles carefully, surprised to find someone working so early in the day.

"Reading a book," muttered Arnold.

"Why do they call you Arnold?" inquired Miles suddenly in fascination.

"Because it's my name," answered Arnold. "Stupid."

"Yes, I see that," said Miles, "but why don't they call you something else? Haven't you got a nickname?"

Arnold shook his head and carried on reading.

"That's bad luck," said Miles sympathetically. "A nickname could do you a lot of good. What did you say you were doing?"

"Reading a book," repeated Arnold with a faint sigh. "Do you mind?"

"Not at all," said Miles. "I like to read a book, especially if it's a good one. It makes me feel good when I've finished it.

41

But that's only if it's a good book. If it's not, then I don't usually finish it, and if I don't finish it I suppose I don't really know whether it was any good or not. Even so, I still feel good because I know I haven't wasted my time reading a book that wasn't any good."

Arnold just tutted. "Stupid."

Miles made a face at him and wandered around the bookshelves, browsing. He turned back abruptly. "Anyway, tell me, Arnold, how is it that you're so clever?"

"I just work at it," came the bored reply. "Tell me, Miles, how is it you're such a lazy good-for-nothing?"

"I just don't work at it," said Miles. "My way is much easier."

Arnold tutted again and turned over another page. "You're mad. Quite mad."

"So I've heard."

Miles sat down and began doodling on the back of yesterday's copy of *The Times*, drawing faces which resembled Arnold. When he had used up most of the space in the margin, he got up and crept over to lock Arnold's briefcase behind his back. It was his favourite pastime, apart from dreaming of bashing Smith. Afterwards, he crept back again to unlock it when he remembered that Arnold had a younger sister in the school who had a friend with nice big tits. He threw the newspaper to one side where somebody could eventually admire all the little faces he had drawn.

"I know what's wrong!" he exclaimed dramatically.

"What?" asked Arnold in a startled voice.

"There's no sanity in this crazy place we call a school. Just look around you."

Arnold looked around but didn't see anything worth looking at because the library was still empty except for Miles and himself. He looked back at Miles with an expression of questioning contempt.

"There's nothing to look at," he said guardedly.

"Precisely! There's nothing to look at, and yet you actually looked all around before you told me there was nothing to look at."

"Are you daft or something?"

"No, I'm not. But you are. I'm the only sane person in the whole place, *that's* what's wrong. Just look around you."

Arnold wasn't going to be caught so easily this time.

"I just did," he said cautiously.

"Oh, all right," relented Miles, "maybe you're not as dumb as I thought you were. But you can see what I'm getting at, can't you? I don't mean look around you literally, I mean look around you metaphorically. *Think*. Don't take it all for granted."

"All what?"

"All that they tell you."

"I see," said Arnold slowly, and resumed reading his book. "Stupid."

Miles sighed. "Case proved, I think."

To Arnold everyone was stupid and Miles was no exception. To Miles everyone was crazy and Arnold was certainly no exception. Arnold was highly intelligent, quick to learn and hard to forget. Most of the teachers liked him because he was highly intelligent and quick to learn. Most of his friends disliked him because he called them stupid. Miles disliked him because he was hard to forget, but liked him because he had a younger sister in the school who had a friend with nice big tits. And for that reason alone, Miles tolerated the part of Arnold's character which made him hard to forget, if only for the simple fact that it had magically turned into an asset.

Arnold was a hard worker. He liked working hard because it made him feel clever, and as he was clever anyway he found it easy to work harder and harder until he decided that he could no longer make himself any more clever. When he had reached the highest level of brilliance, he decided that he would look around for something else to do. He would probably think of getting a girlfriend for an experience with the opposite sex. It would have to be some girl who didn't frighten him, as they mostly did. He wondered what he would have to do, and envied others like Adrian who was good at maths and very good at talking to girls. Arnold wished he could be like Adrian. Perhaps he would ask him for some advice.

Miles hardly ever asked Adrian for advice, even though Adrian was good at maths. He deliberately didn't ask Adrian for advice with his maths because Adrian had a girlfriend called Honey, and Miles loved Honey. He fell in love with her every time he saw her. To make certain that Adrian never found out about his secret passion for her, Miles pretended to ignore her every time he saw her. She had honey-coloured hair and her lovely long legs were the colour of pale honey. She wore an unbuttoned duffle coat over her uniform and black high-heeled boots which made her very hard to ignore. Then one day Miles wondered if all this ignoring her was a bad idea because it might have aroused Adrian's suspicions; perhaps it would be wiser not to ignore her at all but to look at her admiringly like everyone else.

Miles tried to reassure himself that it didn't matter whether Adrian knew or not, because he was never likely to ask him for advice anyway.

All Adrian knew anything about, apart from mathematics or Honey, was rugby football. He played and got himself kicked and scratched and bruised and battered into the ground whilst Honey stood excitedly on the touchline and watched him, cheering loudest of all when he kicked and scratched and bruised somebody else or even battered them into the ground.

Every Wednesday afternoon the sixth form had games. Some of the sixth form took part, but most of them remained in the library and common room or went home early. Miles, Brian and Dave had come up with a very good arrangement. They would tell everyone that they were going to do cross-country running, change into thick sweaters and set off at a brisk pace from the gymnasium, taking a route that led them across the rugby field where a game was in progress in order to annoy Paul Brown, leave the school grounds through a gap in the hedge and set a course that led out into the country. Having achieved that much, and left the school safely behind, they diverted their route and followed a narrow lane which shortly brought them to a small village where they ran straight into its one and only pub.

They usually found Peter there, sitting in a dark corner pretending to be sketching.

"Oh, hello," said Peter in surprise. "What are you doing here?"

"The same as you," they said.

"What, sketching?"

"No, running," said Brian. "It's very thirsty work, all this running. We've been for miles."

"He's there," said Peter, pointing to Miles.

"So he is," said Dave. "Whose round is it this week?"

"Yours," said Miles. "It's been your round for three weeks."

"Damn, I've forgotten to bring any money with me," said Dave, grinning at them.

"How unusual," said Brian, and went to get the drinks instead. Peter finished his own pint with a flourish and smacked his lips.

"You can get me one as well, if you like," he called out. "Thanks, Brian. Very kind of you."

Brian ordered four pints of beer from the sleepy, unobservant landlord who had no idea that he was serving schoolboys, except for the fact that he gave Brian a broad wink and said quietly, "Having a nice run today, sir? It's a fine afternoon for a bit of cross-country." Brian carried the drinks back to the table and set them down.

"Cheers, everyone," said Peter.

They all drank deeply and settled back in contentment. "I like this sort of games lesson," said Miles, gazing up at the ceiling. "Isn't it wonderful that school has so much to offer?"

Peter glanced across at him.

"I don't know why you three bother going, you never do anything."

45

"Well what about you?" said Miles. "What do *you* do all day except mess about in that art room of yours pretending to draw pictures?"

"Ah, but what pictures," said Peter dreamily. "Anyway," he added, "at least it shows I've got an aim in life."

"So have we," said Dave indignantly. "The aim is to do plenty of nothing and make it look like not much of anything."

"Is that supposed to be better?"

"Of course it is. They can't throw you out for doing not much of anything, because that might really mean that you're doing a lot more of something else."

"And are you doing a lot more of something else?"

"Obviously."

"What's that?"

"Nothing."

"I see," said Peter slowly, not seeing at all. "It sounds a funny kind of aim to me. I think I prefer mine."

They carried on drinking for a while in silence. When they had drained their glasses, Miles went off to get a second round. Brian took a packet of cigarettes from his pocket and lit one. He began blowing smoke-rings into the air and watched them changing shape.

"This is the life," he murmured. "Just sit back and listen to your friends arguing. Let's have a look at your drawing, Peter. Is it any good?"

Peter scribbled a few more details with his pencil, did some shading and turned the sketch-pad around for Brian to inspect it. The top sheet was covered in swirls of pencil lines with circles denoting what Brian could only take to be a head and eyes, with two more circles and dots lower down. It looked as if the pencil had got lost on the sheet and spent the afternoon wandering around aimlessly trying to find its way out.

"What is it?" asked Brian faintly.

"I'm calling it 'nakedness'," said Peter.

"That goes without saying," said Brian. "But is it anyone

we know?"

Peter had a habit of asking some of the fifth form girls to sit for him in their spare time and Brian was trying to recognise the face. Miles glanced at it over his shoulder.

"I've got to hand it to you, Pete, old mate," he said. "You get some good-looking girl to pose for you and then you go and insult her with that."

"Don't you like it?" asked Peter, his face falling in disappointment. "I'm relying on these sketches to give me the right expression."

"Do you mean there are more?" said Brian, and turned the pages of the pad. Sure enough, there were five other drawings of a similar nature.

"That's a back view," pointed out Peter.

"Put it away," said Miles. "It's obvious that you're destined for great success in the art world, and I'm truly humbled in the presence of such talent. This is not for the likes of us, Peter. We men of science do not appreciate beauty in the same way as you men of art."

They whiled away a few more minutes in luxurious contemplation of their lives and then the clock behind the bar said it was time for them to be finishing their cross-country run, so Miles, Brian and Dave got up to take their departure, leaving Peter to carry on with his sketching. They were going out through the door when he remembered something and called them back.

"Do you want any tickets for the school dance?"

"When is it?" asked Miles.

"Next week."

"Wasn't it supposed to be last week?"

"Last week it was supposed to be this week."

"And next week it'll be the week after. Why don't you arrange it first and *then* ask us about the tickets."

"Good idea," agreed Dave. "Put me down for two in case I decide to bring Jane."

"Who's Jane?" asked Brian.

"Come to the dance," said Dave, "and you'll find out."

They left Peter to think about the school dance and set off back to school, running with exaggerated tiredness in case anyone was watching out of the classroom windows. They made their way in through the side entrance and trotted around to the gymnasium where they had left their jackets and briefcases. Smith was loitering about in one of the quadrangles and Miles went over to speak to him.

"Hey, Smith," he said cheerfully, "there's somebody over by the back of the hall looking for you."

Smith stared at him through his thick glasses and lifted the corner of his mouth in a sneer.

"Who's looking for me?" he asked.

"I don't know their name," said Miles vaguely. "Why don't you go and find out?"

Smith looked at him again, this time a bit more doubtfully, and walked along the outside of the assembly hall until he was out of sight.

Brian and Dave exchanged glances.

"What are you up to?" said Brian.

"This should give us a little harmless amusement," said Miles. "A diversion of light relief at the end of another long hard day. Give him a minute and then we'll go after him."

"What are you going to do?" asked Dave curiously.

"Wait and find out."

They gave him a minute and then ambled around to the back of the hall. Smith was standing on his own, looking about.

"There's nobody here," he shouted to Miles. "What were you talking about, Randolph?"

"Are you all alone?" cooed Miles. "What a shame. Have you tried looking in the changing room by the gym?"

"No. You didn't say to."

"Come along then. Perhaps your friend has gone in there."

"What friend?" asked Smith.

"Oh, I beg your pardon," said Miles, "I forgot, you haven't got any."

He turned Smith around firmly by the shoulders and

started to propel him over to the open door in the side of the gymnasium. They all went in.

There was nobody in the boys' changing room. Miles didn't think there would be, because he had made it all up. He grinned at Brian and Dave, who were standing in the doorway, and said: "I think it's time we gave Smith a shower, don't you? See if we can get rid of the nasty smell."

"I think that's an excellent idea," said Dave ominously.

"Me too," agreed Brian, and Smith began to look alarmed.

"What are you going to do to me?" he said in a horrified voice.

"We're going to bath you in the showers, that's all," said Miles. "And in case you're wondering why, it's because of what you said in maths the other day about me being in the library."

Smith gave a nervous laugh. "Oh, but that was only a joke!"

"And it was a very funny one," said Miles. "I laughed for ages afterwards. And so is this. When you're sitting under the shower getting yourself soaked, it's only because this is all a big friendly joke. I mean, we *are* all friends, aren't we?"

"Are we?" said Smith feebly.

"Of course we are!" echoed Brian and Dave, advancing towards him. Smith backed over to the far wall by the windows.

"Look, be reasonable," he stammered miserably, turning white in the face. "You can't possibly do this to me. If you do, I'll go straight to the headmaster. He won't be pleased, you know."

"Go ahead," said Brian boldly, "do what you like. We don't care."

In desperation Smith tried to get one of the windows to open.

"You might as well give in and come quietly," said Miles. "Run the water, Dave."

"Hot or cold?" Dave turned on all the taps he could find.

"But what about my clothes?" shrieked Smith. "I can't go

home wet! Whatever will my mother say?"

The water began to cascade in a torrent.

"All right," said Miles, satisfied.

"How are you going to get me over there?" asked Smith defiantly.

"We can either pick you up and throw you in," said Miles, "or we can push you in from here."

They got ready to pounce.

"Why doesn't he save us the bother of having to pick him up and carry him, and jump in of his own accord?" suggested Brian. "Then perhaps we won't beat him up afterwards."

"Beat me up afterwards?" repeated Smith, his eyes nearly popping out of his head. In sudden panic, he ran around the side of them, took a flying leap off the edge of the floor and went sliding under the shower. With hardly a pause he slithered to a halt, scrambled to his feet and raced for the door, water dripping from him everywhere.

"Did you see that?" said Dave in amazement.

"Whatever will his mother say?" gasped Brian.

"He must be crazy," said Miles. "Did he really think I was going to push him in?"

"Weren't you?" said Brian and Dave together.

Miles gave them both a disdainful, almost pitying look. "Do you seriously think I would contaminate myself by laying my hands on that miserable little twit? I wouldn't even touch him with a barge-pole, except for the temptation to shove it up him."

After they had changed their sweaters and collected their bags, they strolled down to the playing field to watch the rest of the rugby match. There was a small group of teachers and sixth-formers standing on the edge of the grass embankment overlooking the pitch and Peter was among them.

"How did you get back so quickly?" demanded Brian.

"I walked," said Peter truthfully. "How did you get back so slowly?"

"We ran," said Miles, just as truthfully, and decided that one of them must be telling lies. He looked around to see if he could spot Honey anywhere. Instead, he noticed the headmaster standing next to one of the youngest female members of staff. The headmaster seemed completely unaware of the intense interest that she was causing to the other spectators and most of the players, for he was more interested in the game than in his companion and it did not even appear to occur to him that the only reason for the players' distraction was the fact that she was standing at the top of the embankment wearing the shortest skirt imaginable. Each of the players seemed to be taking it in turn to fall on the ground next to the touchline and look upwards. Miles decided to join in the fun. He waited for the final whistle and, at the right moment after the players had left the field and the spectators were beginning to disperse, he grabbed hold of Peter and wrestled him to the ground. Peter was too surprised to realise what was happening, but the next thing he knew he was rolling down the steep slope of the embankment with Miles alongside.

"Terribly sorry," said Miles. "I slipped."

He lay on the ground looking up at the sky, waiting. A few seconds later, the teacher appeared at the top, looking over to see what had happened. Miles grinned up at her.

"We slipped, miss," he called up.

"Are you both all right?" inquired the lady teacher.

"Never felt better, thank you, miss," said Miles. Peter was already on his feet, brushing mud and grass off his clothes.

"Aren't you going to get up?" asked the teacher.

"I will in a minute, miss," said Miles, "I've just got to get my breath back." He started coughing and spluttering. "Christ!" he muttered to himself, "pink frilly knickers!"

Chapter 6

If there was a secret to Miles's success in not doing any work, it was to make its avoidance difficult to notice. Therefore he did not have a routine of complete idleness, but varied it from day to day as the mood took him, or as expediency dictated. Sometimes he went to lessons because he wanted to, sometimes he went because he thought it would be a bit of fun – after all, nothing becomes so tedious as being constantly idle in one place. He liked to see different parts of the school, he enjoyed watching others working hard and he took pleasure in helping the staff to do their job without realising that, in his case, their efforts were being entirely wasted.

On Tuesday mornings he usually went to the chemistry practical lesson. It was a temptation to his nihilistic nature that he could handle all the chemicals he would ever need to blow up the school and it satisfied his sense of superiority that the matter of life-and-death should be in his hands and that he was the one to decide on the outcome.

"You only go to chem. prac. because you fancy the lab assistant," said Brian, who found chemistry practicals very confusing.

"I can think of no better reason for going," admitted Miles. Actually there were two assistants who were responsible for looking after the chemistry, physics and biology laboratories. One of them was tall, fair-haired and beautiful and reminded them of a Nordic goddess, so they called her Helga. The other was short, fat and ugly, with dark straight hair, who dressed in a lab coat which was stiff and unyielding, so they called her Miss Starch. "Or no worse reason," he added when he thought about her.

"There must be another reason," said Dave brightly.

"There is," said Miles. "I happen to be in the middle of a very interesting experiment."

The chemistry practical lesson began immediately after assembly and went on all morning. Everyone who took A-level chemistry had to own a white laboratory coat which they wore over their usual school uniform to protect it from the harmful effect of accidentally-spilled chemicals, and Miles carried his coat in his briefcase, taking it to school only when he needed it. So did Brian and Dave. Most of the others in his class left their coats hanging up on pegs behind the door for the rest of the week.

The lab was empty when they arrived and they immediately took out their coats and put them on. They usually left them unbuttoned since it looked more impressive, walking around with the coat flapping open, hands in pockets. In Miles's opinion it appeared almost professorial and he frequently took a walk around the school to show whoever cared to look that he was rather important. By the time he got back to the laboratory, everyone else was busy working and Mr Farley, the chemistry master, was sitting behind his desk, wearing his own immaculate white lab coat over a checked sports jacket and light grey flannel trousers. He had a long pointed face, a furrowed brow and beady blue eyes that missed nothing. Chemistry was a popular subject and there were twenty-five boys and girls in his class, divided between two long laboratory benches. Miles, Brian and Dave usually worked at the back of the lab, where they could mess around without being noticed. Miles led the way around to their place, and when he passed Barbara, who was bending forward to inspect the level of hydrochloric acid in her burette, he gave her a teasing smack on the bottom. She squeaked and he grinned at her. This gave Brian an idea, and he did the same thing only in his enthusiasm he managed to do it much harder, almost knocking her over. She gave a shrill cry and turned on him with a furious glare.

"Cheek!" she squealed and slapped his face. The grin he had been preparing froze into a horrified gape, and Miles and Dave dragged him away. They buttoned up their lab coats and got themselves ready for the lesson.

"Ah, Randolph. Er, Miles," said Mr Farley, coming over to them and giving Miles his fearful one-sided smile which meant that he was in the mood to see some work done. "What are you doing this week?"

"Same as last week, sir," said Miles.

"Oh yes. And what's that?"

"I wasn't here last week, sir," confessed Miles.

"I see," said Mr Farley slowly, who was never reluctant to share a joke. "Er, does that mean you don't intend to do anything?"

"Oh no, sir, I wasn't doing *nothing* last week," explained Miles. "By that I mean I was doing *something*, even if it wasn't a chemistry practical."

"So what was the last experiment you did?"

"It was the one I didn't finish, sir."

"You'd better finish it today, then."

"Yes, sir, I was thinking I'd better. After all, if I don't finish it I might never know how to do it, and then what if I get it in the exam, sir? It's always possible, isn't it?"

Mr Farley increased the fearfulness of his one-sided smile.

"I do like to see enthusiasm," he said.

"I know, sir. My two friends here are just as enthusiastic as I am," said Miles. Brian and Dave grinned and nodded enthusiastically. They were looking forward to a good long morning of playing about.

"What experiment are you finishing?" asked Mr Farley.

Miles had no idea, he had forgotten. He quickly picked up an experiment card from the bench nearby – the first to come to hand – looked at it and said, "Ah, this one."

"Hey, I'm doing that," protested a voice along the bench. It was Billy, whose real name was Robert Marshall, but he looked like a billy-goat. "Give it back."

"Shut your face," said Miles self-righteously in a low and threatening voice.

Billy opened his mouth to protest even more. "No I won't! Oooof!" Miles dug his elbow in Billy's stomach whilst Mr Farley was examining the card and put his foot out behind so that he went flying backwards and ended up on the floor. A stool crashed over with him.

They all gazed at him.

"He fell over, sir," said Miles blandly, and they all turned away again while Billy picked himself up.

"What are you doing?" Mr Farley asked Brian.

"The same as him, sir," said Brian, pointing to Miles.

"And what are you doing?" he asked Dave.

"The same as him, sir," said Dave, pointing to Brian.

And with a great deal of fuss they started to get their bits and pieces of apparatus together. Burettes, pipettes, conical flasks, beakers of various sizes, test tubes – they all came out on the bench, followed by bottles of acid, bottles of alkali, litmus and pH paper, powdered chemicals, distilled water, spatulas for sampling, funnels for pouring and glass rods for stirring. Their end of the room saw the most activity and produced the least results, except when something went wrong.

Dave could never do any of the experiments without getting hopelessly stuck or breaking some of the expensive apparatus or somehow making a lethal mixture out of the most harmless of the laboratory's contents. One day he left a bottle of ether standing without its glass stopper next to a roaring bunsen burner. A minute later there were flames all over the place and a fire extinguisher had to be used. On another occasion he struggled through a particularly difficult experiment which should have been easy enough except that he hadn't the slightest notion of what he was doing, when suddenly he found himself releasing a cloud of pungent brown gas into the laboratory. Everyone had to be evacuated immediately, amidst much coughing and gasping for breath, and he proudly discovered that he had just learned how to make bromine. After that unfortunate episode they threatened to make him work in the fume cupboard.

"I don't know why I ever wanted to take chemistry," he wailed miserably. "All it ever does is go wrong."

"It's fun," said Miles encouragingly, and went for a walk around the laboratory to see how everyone else was getting on, especially the girls.

Smith was forever prominent, screwing up his nasty little face to make out he was stuck and in great difficulty whereas in fact he was exactly the opposite in his own irritating way. He was always one of the first to finish an experiment and would then go around smirking secretively at the rest of the class.

"How is it you always finish so quickly, Smith?" asked Miles. "Looked in the book, did you, to see all the answers?"

Several others nearby began to snigger.

Smith went red in the face and fiddled with his glasses. Glancing around the lab, he said in a loud voice, "Been to maths lately, Randolph?"

Miles picked up a plastic wash-bottle from the bench. It contained distilled water. He squeezed it and a fine jet of water squirted out and hit Smith in the face. He howled and Miles went back to his own part of the room.

"Now, what experiment are we doing?" he demanded, and Brian consulted the card.

"It's a tit ration," came the answer after a moment.

"That sounds promising," said Miles. "How much of a ration, and whose?"

"It doesn't say."

"Come here, give me the card." Miles snatched it out of Brian's hand and looked at it. "It's titration, you idiot!"

"There's a gap between the *t* and the *r*," protested Brian, and showed him.

"I hate titrations," said Dave irritably. "Can't we do something else?"

"Like what?" said Miles.

"We could make some gunpowder," he suggested darkly, "and then we could blow up the lab."

"Too much trouble," said Miles dismissively, so they pretended to get on with the titration experiment. By the end of the morning all they had done was keep Helga running around for them. She knew they only did it because they fancied her and she played up to them. Occasionally she even opened her lab coat to flaunt her tight black jumper at them when nobody else was looking. Miles was always trying to ask her out and she showed her satisfaction of his attentiveness by pretending to be strict and disapproving. He never knew whether she was being strict and disapproving because she liked pretending to hide her satisfaction of his attentiveness or whether she thought he wasn't being attentive enough to meet with her satisfaction.

"I don't know why I do everything for the three of you all the time," she said, lighting a bunsen burner for them. "You are helpless."

"We didn't know where the lighter was," said Miles innocently. "What are you doing tonight?"

She wrinkled her pretty nose at them and walked off to another part of the lab, leaving them to stand in awe of her trim slender figure.

"It shouldn't be allowed," said Miles.

"What shouldn't be allowed?" asked Brian.

"Letting a girl like that work here."

"You're crazy," said Dave.

"I can't help it."

When the bell rang for breaktime, everyone removed their lab coats, except for Miles, Brian and Dave who liked to show off in theirs, and left the laboratory to spend their fifteen-minute break in the sixth form common room or the library or meandering around the school. Mr Farley disappeared to the staff room. Helga usually made a cup of coffee for herself in the storeroom and if Miss Starch was on duty, she had a liking for Chelsea buns and gobbled up a bagful with her own supply of butter and strawberry jam. Sometimes Miles found that he was enjoying himself so much with his experiment that he simply had to carry on with it.

One day he decided to conduct an experiment that was not listed in Mr Farley's cards.

"What are we going to do?" asked Dave, rubbing his hands together in anticipation.

"It's an experiment to test the durability of fabric," explained Miles. "It's perfectly straightforward." He ran his eye over the shelves and took down a bottle marked *"Nitric Acid (concentrated)"*. Then he rummaged through the lab coats hanging on the back of the door, took one down from its peg and stuffed it into a drawer which he pulled out from the long laboratory workbench. With a flourish, he picked up the bottle of acid, took off the glass stopper and poured its contents into the drawer. Then he slammed the drawer shut and replaced the empty bottle on its shelf.

Five minutes later they heard footsteps outside in the corridor and the door opened to admit the rest of the class. They arrived in ones and twos, settled at their usual places and got ready for the rest of the morning's lesson. The lab coats quickly disappeared off the pegs as they put them back on. Miles, Brian and Dave waited expectantly.

A sneering face turned from the empty row of pegs with a puzzled expression.

"Has anyone seen my lab coat?" asked Smith.

Twenty-one other faces in the class looked up at him and there was a general shaking of heads to show that they had not. Three others sat grinning at him.

"All right, what have you done with it?" he asked Miles.

"Are you sure you didn't take it home with you?" inquired Miles. "Perhaps it needed a wash."

"I did *not* take it home with me," said Smith. "I was wearing it earlier and left it here at the start of break. Now where is it?"

Miles, Brian and Dave turned their eyes in unison from

Smith to the closed drawer. He followed the direction of their gaze and, with an exasperated look on his face, walked around the long bench. He reached forward, pulled on the handle and opened the drawer.

At first, nobody could comprehend what had happened. It looked to begin with as though Miles had accomplished a very clever disappearing trick, for there was no sign of the lab coat. Instead, faint wisps of white smoke drifted up and there was rather a pungent odour. Smith's lab coat had not so much disappeared as dissolved, transmogrified into thin air, and the only thing that remained of it at the bottom of the drawer was a shred of fabric and four buttons.

"Oh dear," said Miles. "Did you leave it in there?"

Everybody else in the laboratory burst out laughing. Smith went red in the face, glared at Miles, picked up his briefcase and walked out. He had, after all, finished his experiment.

"It was obviously Miss Starch," said Miles. "Smith repelled her advances and this is her revenge." And so it was that Smith's lab coat and Miss Starch became a part of school folklore. Nor could Smith prove anything to the contrary, for when he eventually went back to the lab, the last bit of cloth had vanished and so had the buttons. His coat had well and truly evaporated, gone up in a puff of reeking white smoke. The bottom of the drawer stayed hot for the rest of the morning.

Chapter 7

There were rare occasions when Miles's conscience got the better of him and he went along to visit the careers master, who sat in his small paper-littered den in a small annexe beside the sixth form common room when he wasn't teaching mathematics to the remedial section of the lower school, who could be so obtuse that it seemed a pointless waste of time. He often set them simple problems and escaped up to his little hideaway where few people bothered him.

Everyone called him Minus Davies because it was assumed that he must be lacking in any form of sense to want to be a careers master as well as a remedial mathematician. He secretly gloried in his nickname because of its mathematical connotation and felt that it was like being awarded a medal.

Minus Davies was a pleasant little man with a rosy-red, well-scrubbed little face and sleek black hair smoothed down with pomade. He was slight and dapper in build, wore a dark, expensively-tailored suit and had a distinctly unteacherly aspect to his nature, speaking with a gentle Welsh accent. He could sympathise and empathise with the boys and girls in his charge, he could conspire with them and understand their problems.

Whenever Miles paid him a visit in his tiny lair, Minus Davies always told him that there was no future for those who had not established a past, and Miles invariably went to the trouble of applying the opposite – that there was no past for those who did not want to establish a future. He pondered on this gravely and came to the conclusion that he had plenty of past so why bother to worry? Miles just decided that Minus Davies must be completely off his head and this was sufficient reason for Miles to start taking him seriously.

"You must work," said Minus Davies.

"I know, sir."

"I'm always telling pupils that if they don't work, they won't get anywhere in this world of ours. You *must* work."

"Of course I must, sir."

"And work hard. It's no good just working, that's not enough. You must work *hard*."

Miles nodded distantly.

"Tell me, now, what do you want to do when you leave school?"

Miles sighed happily and gazed into space.

"I'd like to pursue my present interests, sir," he said.

"That's excellent. Excellent. What exactly are your present interests?"

Miles decided to try and make a special effort. He thought about Suzanne, he thought about Francesca and he thought about Honey. They passed through his mind together with all the other nameless girls he fancied, but he decided that this was not the sort of answer his careers master wanted to hear.

"Well, sir, I'm hoping to develop a keen sense of preservation. Preservation, that is, for my present interests."

"Oh yes, of course," said Minus Davies, "that sounds like a very wise idea, if you want to know what I think. Um, what are your present interests again?"

Miles sniffed.

"I always wanted to be a doctor, sir."

Minus Davies sat forward keenly in his chair.

"That's a *very* good idea, if you want to know what I think," he said.

"Yes, sir."

"You *do* want to know what I think, don't you?"

"Naturally, sir."

"A *very* good idea is what *I* think."

"Yes, sir," said Miles mechanically. Trouble is, though, sir, you cocked it up for me, you and the rest of the school, he thought.

"What particular reason did you have for wanting to be a doctor?" asked Minus Davies with great interest and indifference whilst he sorted through some papers on his desk.

"I suppose I just decided it's what I wanted to do, sir."

"Mmmmm?"

"I mean, I suppose I just wanted to be a doctor without having a particular reason, sir. Does there have to be a reason?"

"Oh yes!" said Minus Davies emphatically. "There must always be a reason for everything."

"Yes, sir."

"That's philosophy."

"I imagine it is, sir."

"Nothing happens without a cause. Mark my words, without a cause, nothing happens."

"I just wanted to be a doctor, sir."

If Miles could sit there and plumb unknown depths of philosophical conjecture in the mind of his careers master, then it shouldn't be too hard for him to persuade Suzanne to go out with him. The thought pleased him.

"How are you getting on with your work?" asked Minus Davies suddenly.

Miles considered the question.

"Oh, pretty well, I'd say, sir," he replied.

"Do you have any problems you'd like to talk about? I'm only here to try and help, so if you do have any problems of any kind, you can feel as free as you like to talk about them."

Miles thought about it.

"No, I don't think I've got any particular problems, sir," he said.

"That's good, then, isn't it?"

"Yes," agreed Miles gloomily, "I suppose it is."

"And if you have any problems in the future, don't hesitate to come and talk to me about them."

"That's very kind of you, sir. Thank you very much."

Miles became aware that Minus Davies was staring blankly into the air with a detached look in his eyes, so he got up to go. Without another word being spoken, he pushed the chair back in place and left the room. He wondered why he had ever wanted to be a doctor, it just didn't seem to make any sense. Not any more. He wandered off to the library.

Brian was worried, so he went to see Minus Davies. He arrived only five minutes after Miles had left.

"I was just thinking of you a moment ago," fibbed Minus Davies hospitably, welcoming Brian into the hideaway.

"Why not think of something else?" suggested Brian, and made Minus Davies think of the day he became careers master so that he could lock himself away in his small room and forget about teaching mathematics to the remedial section of the lower school who didn't want to learn it anyway.

"You've got a problem," hinted Minus Davies, who knew all there was to know about problems. "I want you to tell me all about it, because a problem shared is a problem halved."

"Not if you had my problem," said Brian miserably.

"But I haven't got your problem," Minus Davies reminded him, "so why don't you tell me about it?"

"The problem," said Brian, "is overwork. Obviously I'm working too hard and I don't even realise the effect it's having on me. I don't think I ever appreciated that the possibility of overwork existed with me, but it does."

"Take time off to study your conscience," prescribed Minus Davies, and Brian took the advice gratefully.

"Thank you, sir," he said.

"Did I ever tell you what happened when a boy asked me if he could become a hospital matron?" asked Minus Davies vaguely.

"No," said Brian, "I don't think you did tell me what happened."

"Oh," said Minus Davies, and gazed into the atmosphere. "I don't think I told anyone what happened. Not even the headmaster, and he didn't want to know anyway because he's got problems of his own."

"Has he, sir?" said Brian politely.

Minus Davies snorted. "Mind you, his problems are nothing to the ones *I've* got."

"Aren't they, sir?" said Brian sympathetically.

"Of course not! Nothing at all! What about the time when a girl came to me for advice?" said Minus Davies. "*I* couldn't give her *that* sort of advice. I told her she needed to see a doctor. Even the headmaster needs to see a doctor but he refuses to let the deputy think he's going to. But the deputy's bound to find out sooner or later. Why don't you ask the headmaster if he'll let you take time to study your conscience? He can't afford not to."

Minus Davies could be a mine of information when the mood suited him, and it suited him most of the time because he was a cynic at heart and delighted in pulling people's egos apart bit by bit. The headmaster was already the hopeless victim of his latest denouement by having the poor unfortunate pregnant girl sent down to see him under the impression that she was going to see one of the mistresses who dealt kindly with such matters. Minus Davies had a wicked sense of humour and nobody knew anything about it. He knew that he could be entirely corrupt if he wanted to be, but he didn't want to be. Instead, he only wanted to keep pulling people's egos apart with dreadful subtlety.

"Why bother to work at all?" he argued expansively. "I wanted to be an astro-physicist once and look where the ambition got me in the end. It's one of the absurdities of modern civilisation, did you know that?"

"I always suspected it, sir," said Brian wisely.

Minus Davies nodded his satisfaction. "Don't let them make you do anything you don't want to do," he insisted.

"I won't," decided Brian and grinned broadly. "Sir, what would happen if *nobody* worked?"

"That's for you to find out," said Minus Davies. "I'm too old for that sort of thing now."

Brian went to see the headmaster in his study, where he was hiding from two troublesome parents whilst the deputy escorted them across the lobby to his own room and asked Francesca to fetch three cups of tea from the canteen even though the two troubled parents insisted that they didn't want any.

"I always drink three cups of tea in the afternoon," said the deputy, "with plenty of sugar."

He sent Francesca back to the canteen to fetch plenty of sugar. When she got back to the office, the headmaster was brooding in his study while Brian slipped in quietly and asked him if he could take time to study his conscience.

"Don't think *you've* got problems," scoffed the headmaster scornfully. "What about me? I've got nothing but problems."

"What kind of problems have you got, sir?" asked Brian.

"What?" demanded the headmaster.

"Didn't say anything, sir," said Brian, startled.

"Oh. I thought you did."

"No, sir, I didn't say a thing."

"If I didn't have any problems I'd be a good headmaster," vowed the headmaster.

"If you were a good headmaster you wouldn't have any problems," echoed Brian reciprocally.

"I haven't got any problems at all," said the headmaster hurriedly. "Not one. Not a single problem. Not even the slightest bit of a problem."

"What kind of problems haven't you got, sir?" asked Brian, trying a different approach.

"What?" demanded the headmaster.

"Didn't say anything, sir," said Brian, startled.

"Oh. I thought you did."

"No, sir, I still didn't say a thing. Can I have time to study my conscience, please, sir?"

"Why?" inquired the headmaster. "Is it likely to be of any benefit to the running of the school?"

"It might be," reckoned Brian, not untruthfully.

"Good," said the headmaster. "Take as much time as you like, and tell me in future when you're going to say anything."

"Yes, sir. Of course, sir. Do you know Mr Davies, sir? It was he who suggested I should come and ask you."

"Who's Mr Davies?" asked the headmaster mysteriously.

"The careers master, sir. It appears that nobody seems to know him."

"Do *I* know him?" demanded the headmaster.

"I don't know, sir," said Brian. "Only you know whether you know him or not."

"I don't, then," decided the headmaster. "What about him? Is there something I should know?"

"He knows you, sir."

"Well, I wish he didn't," grumbled the headmaster. "Maybe I'd be a better headmaster if everyone left me alone."

"I thought you said you didn't have any problems, sir," said Brian, and went off to look for some nice girls to try and pick up.

Chapter 8

One morning, after weeks of waiting for the opportunity, Miles at last managed to borrow his old man's car for school. It so happened that on exactly the same morning Dave got his hands on his mother's little old green Mini and gave Brian a lift to school in it. He bravely steered it all the way from his home on the opposite side of town, in and out of the busy morning traffic with Brian sitting alongside feeling very important, turned in at the school gates, made his way up the drive and parked it carefully in a small space behind the kitchens, next to the rubbish bins.

He and Brian got out, and Dave had the self-satisfied look on his face of one who has pulled off no small achievement, when the sound of another car made them both turn. A gleaming white Rover 3500 approached up the drive, swung around in the yard and came to a halt alongside them. Miles jumped out and grinned at them.

"Morning, boys," he said with an even greater look of self-satisfaction on his face. "Where did you get that rusting heap of crap from?"

"This happens to be my mother's car," said Dave indignantly, "and it's in very good nick."

Miles glowed with the feeling of inner warmth that was going to be difficult to dampen. He inclined his head towards the bins. "I'd have said you'd be better off in one of those," he remarked with a supercilious smirk.

Dave aimed a punch at him but he dodged out of the way

in time.

"Dave's a very good driver," said Brian. "We only just missed having two crashes."

"What do you mean?" demanded Dave. "Where?"

"One was at the traffic lights, when you went over on red," said Brian, enjoying himself, "and the other was when you overtook the bus."

"What was wrong with that?"

"There was a big Pickfords lorry coming the other way."

"Well, I missed it, didn't I?" said Dave. "And I got you here in one piece."

"That was only because I was praying hard," said Brian ruefully. He turned to Miles with an envious expression. "Nice motor."

Miles took his briefcase from the back seat, closed the rear door gently with his elbow and locked the driver's door. Dave walked all around it in a daze.

"Can we go for a ride in it?" asked Brian suddenly.

"Oh, I see," said Dave, his voice rising. "So my little Mini isn't good enough for you any longer, is it?"

"Has it got a radio?" asked Miles.

"No, it hasn't got a radio," said Dave.

"Mine has," said Miles. "Has it got a stereo cassette?"

"No, it hasn't got a stereo cassette," said Dave in exasperation.

"Mine has," sang Miles.

"How about going for a ride in it?" said Brian again. "Come on, I can't wait."

"Later," suggested Miles.

"Why not now?" said Brian.

"Why not later?" countered Miles. "At dinnertime. We'll give Dave a race."

The matter was settled.

"How did you manage to persuade your old man to let you borrow his car?" asked Dave.

"He's working abroad for a few days," said Miles.

"Didn't your mother mind?" asked Brian.

"She has one quality above all others," said Miles seraphically. "Virtue."

"My old lady's so virtuous that she refuses to drive around in a car that hasn't passed its MOT," said Dave.

Brian viewed him askance, quite shocked.

"*What?* Do you mean that old thing has failed its test?" he yelled.

"No, I didn't mean that at all," said Dave. "It happens to be a very good car. It just hasn't got an MOT, that's all."

"That's against the law," said Miles self-righteously.

"Well, it has *really*," confessed Dave. "You don't honestly think I'd drive around in a car that hasn't got an MOT, do you?"

"I wouldn't be surprised," said Miles.

Brian was struggling to keep up with the argument. "If I don't honestly think you'd drive around in a car that hasn't got an MOT," he said, "how is it that you're driving around in a car without an MOT?"

"It *has* got an MOT!" shouted Dave.

"You said it hasn't," protested Brian.

"I didn't. I said my old dear is so virtuous that she refuses to drive around in a car if it hasn't passed its test. *She* doesn't think it's passed because I told her it hasn't, but *I* know it has so that's why I'm driving around in it."

There was a stunned silence.

"That's deceitful," said Miles in a respectful whisper.

Dave merely smiled. "I reckon I can't help it," he said.

Miles's white Rover caused a great deal of interest around the school from the moment it appeared. Word quickly spread about it but nobody knew to whom it belonged. They went in groups to look at it during breaktime, walking all around it, peering in through the windows at the dark leather interior. It made most of the teachers' cars look like old wrecks, which the majority of them were anyway, rather like the Mini that was parked next to it. The teachers themselves were puzzled by its appearance.

When the headmaster heard that there was a new car in the

school that no one seemed to know anything about, he sent the deputy to investigate. When the deputy heard that there was a new car in the school that no one knew anything about, he immediately detected a lie. If he knew about it, he only knew because the headmaster already knew himself. So the deputy went to investigate. By the time he got there it had gone because Miles had no wish for the deputy to see it. He took Brian and Dave for a lunchtime spin in it and they drove recklessly around Kingshampton's town centre, breaking all the speed limits. It had a big engine with eight cylinders and went very fast. Miles sat nonchalantly at the wheel, resting his arm on the open window, Brian sat alongside in the passenger seat and Dave lolled about in the back.

"Nice car," said Brian admiringly. "Let's go looking for girls."

"What about that race we were meant to be having?" said Dave, thinking of his Mini.

Miles pressed his foot down harder on the accelerator pedal and the car surged forward with a powerful roar from its three-and-a-half litre engine.

"If this was a race," he said, "you'd still be making your way down the drive."

Brian watched the dials on the dashboard in awe. The big needles swept around in response to their rising speed and Miles was obviously enjoying himself. They left the town centre and headed out onto the by-pass road. The midday traffic was light and Miles hurtled past it at an ever-increasing velocity until the road brought them around to the far end of town where he turned back towards the centre. They slowed down again and made more stately progress into the main streets, looking at all the pretty girls walking along the pavements. Suddenly Dave sat up in the back.

"There's Jane!" he exclaimed. "Stop the car!"

Miles swung in towards the kerb and pulled up dramatically.

"Toot the horn," said Dave. Miles obliged. Several

pedestrians turned around to look. Dave quickly wound his window down and leaned out of the car. He put two fingers in his mouth and gave a piercing whistle which made even more people look around in surprise.

"Where is she?" asked Miles, peering through the windscreen.

"She's gone up there," said Dave, pointing to a side street. "She didn't look. Let's get after her, come on!"

"I can't see any girl," said Miles. "What does she look like?"

"Beautiful," said Dave rapturously.

"I can't see any girl either," said Brian. "I think you imagined her."

"I imagine her all the time," said Dave blissfully. "Come on, let's go, quickly!"

Miles obligingly put his foot down hard on the accelerator and the Rover roared away from the kerb. He spun the steering wheel and they turned into a narrow street with tall old buildings and high walls on either side. It led into another part of the main thoroughfare. There was no sign of any young girl walking along, beautiful or otherwise. They turned again into a one-way street that took them to the town's market square. There were plenty of people about, and many of them were young women, but there was nobody that Dave could recognise. He slumped back in his seat.

"We've missed her," he said lugubriously.

"There are lots of ugly freaks around," said Miles unkindly. "Are you sure she's not one of them?"

"When you meet Jane, you'll realise that she's probably the most beautiful girl you have ever seen in your lives," said Dave dreamily.

"*If* she exists," said Brian, who had a suspicion that Jane was nothing more than a figment of Dave's imagination, like the drinking sessions in the pub. These were, in fact, the bombastic and inflated ramblings of a prize show-off, he decided, the fantasy of a deluded mind. In his own thoughts he wanted to have a girl like Jane, a gorgeous pin-up hanging

71

possessively onto his arm, and he began to feel depressed. But Miles blew away the clouds of gathering misery by deciding that he had had enough of chasing after an elusive shadow. He turned the car around in the middle of the square with a flick of the wheel and they were off again, building up to a tremendous speed that took their breath away. It was reckless driving and they loved every minute of it. They circled Kingshampton again, approached the centre from a different direction, took off along another road and eventually, as with the most exhilarating fairground ride, came to the end of it – the clock on the dashboard told them that it was time to return to school. Miles parked in the space beside Dave's Mini, guessing that by now everyone, including the deputy, would have lost interest in the appearance of the new unknown car.

"That was a most enjoyable ride," said Brian. "Thanks very much, Miles. I'd say it was almost as enjoyable as the ride I had this morning, with the near-certainty of a collision at every turn."

"I do my best to please," said Miles happily.

"That's what Jane said to me once," sighed Dave. "Only hers was a softer ride, and she didn't roll as much. Hey, what are you doing, boys? Stop it! I was only joking!"

Miles and Brian dragged him out of the car and started beating him up, but he only began to laugh helplessly.

"Come on, boys, give it a rest!"

"This girl Jane you keep telling us about," said Miles, "you've made her all up, haven't you? *Haven't* you?"

"She doesn't exist, does she?" said Brian. "*Does* she?"

"All right, all right!" said Dave. "Stop it!"

"Do you admit it?" said Miles.

"I admit it!"

"You'll never mention her name again?"

"I'll never mention her name again," promised Dave, trying to keep a straight face. "Sorry, boys, but it's so funny."

"What is?" asked Brian suspiciously.

"The look on your silly faces. I'm sorry, but I can't stop

laughing."

He was still sniggering when they went back into school and neither Miles nor Brian knew what had got into him. They spent the afternoon in the library, where Dave soon fell asleep as usual. Brian took out his chemistry file and began gazing at it until the words and chemical symbols became one large meaningless blur, whilst Miles took out a notebook and began making up silly rhymes. His first effort went like this:

There was a young boy called Dave
Who didn't know how to behave
So all of his friends
Said "If you don't make amends
There'll be nothing of you left to save."

He read it through, nodded in satisfaction and decided that he had found a new pastime to help pass the time.

Chapter 9

One morning Dave arrived in school bright and early with his latest idea. He parked his mother's Mini in what had become its usual place and, instead of making his way up to the library, he went along to the physics laboratory and settled himself into the small storage room at the back where anyone was allowed to go and study in peace and quiet at any time of the day as long as none of the physics teachers minded, which they never did. It was known as the darkroom because its window had a large black blind which could be pulled down to put the room in total darkness in order for certain experiments involving prisms, lenses and a lightbox to be performed, and at the far end of a workbench stood a photographic enlarger, developing tank and chemicals; it was once rumoured that Mr Parks the senior physics master had taken pictures of a sixth form girl and sold them to a glossy magazine for a lot of money, although Dave had his doubts about the truthfulness of such a story. Mr Parks was a keen ornithologist and it seemed more likely that a feathered bird had popped obligingly out of the bushes for him and not Michelle the tall, stunningly-beautiful raven-haired girl who got away with coming to school in black fishnet tights and four-inch heels. Still, you could never be sure with some of these respectable middle-aged teachers. And he was reputed to have a long one. Lens, that is. Dave shook his head at the thought.

There was a table and stools at one end of the room and

shelves stacked high with experimental equipment at the other. An ancient epidiascope stood on the floor in the far corner beside a dusty old 16mm sound projector used by the film club. Dave noticed the electrostatic generator standing harmlessly in the opposite corner and made a nasty face at it. Then he had another thought, went over to it and pretended to punch it. His fist connected accidentally with the large polished dome, which let out a loud metallic clang and the contraption rocked dangerously. He flinched away with a howl of pain, nursing his sore knuckles and swearing under his breath at it in case anyone outside the room had heard. He ran his eye over all the other intriguing pieces of apparatus.

When Brian eventually came wandering in, Dave was playing with an electronic calculator which had been left lying on a side bench. He was marvelling at the way it could do its sums and get them right every time.

Brian looked at the books that Dave had got out of his case and were now arranged in front of him.

"What are you doing?" he asked with mild curiosity.

"Working, of course," said Dave.

"What do you mean, *of course?* I haven't seen you do any work for months, and certainly not physics."

"Well if it comes to that, I haven't seen *you* do any work for months either," replied Dave in a haughty voice. "But that doesn't necessarily mean that if you happened to tell me one day that you were working I would immediately turn around and laugh it off with deep and utter scepticism. I just wouldn't believe you either."

"So you're not really working at all?" said Brian persistently.

"No."

Brian breathed a sigh of relief. "Thank heavens for that. I thought for one moment there was something wrong with you."

"Never fear," said Dave, "I'm still perfectly sane, unlike some people around here." He waved the matter aside. He remembered a new contrivance he had thought up which could only be used safely in the physics darkroom. He dived down into his briefcase and pulled out a long coiled length of clear plastic tubing.

"What's that for?" asked Brian, peering at it.

"It's my latest idea," explained Dave. He bent down to his case again and this time he produced a can of beer.

"Christ, what have you got there?" gargled Brian, his voice rising to a high-pitched squeak.

Dave put a finger to his lips for silence and pulled the metal ring on the top of the can. It opened with a sudden release of gas and he peeled the ring away. The smell of beer wafted up to his nose and had the same effect as good music to the ear. He dipped one end of the plastic tube into the hole in the top of the can and carefully placed the can upright inside his briefcase. Then he took hold of the other end of the tube and pulled it up his sleeve until it reached his shoulder, where he drew it out and put it in his mouth. He began sucking. Beer flowed up the tube in a thin brown line and he swallowed it with a pleasurable expression on his face. He sank his head down into his books and the tube was now barely visible.

"Mmmmm," he murmured happily. "Want some?"

"Course I do," said Brian. "Come here, give me a suck."

"I wouldn't wish to take that remark the wrong way," teased Dave, and received a mild punch on the arm. Brian snatched the tube from him and drank quickly.

"We could get pissed like this," he muttered after a moment.

"Well, *you're* not going to!" retorted Dave and grabbed it back again.

They fell into a thoughtful silence.

"Are you going to the school dance?" inquired Brian at last.

"When is it?" asked Dave.

"Next week, according to Peter."

Dave nodded. "Of course I'm going. How about you?"

"I want a girl," said Brian dramatically.

"Do you?"

"Yes! I want to have a good screw."

Dave gulped and broke out in a fit of coughing.

"I don't think it's going to be one of *those* dances," he said hurriedly.

"Why not?" demanded Brian. "Peter's organising it, isn't he?"

"I imagine so."

"There you are, then."

The door of the darkroom opened unexpectedly and Brian glanced up to see Helga the lab assistant appearing. He watched her enter the room and thought that she looked like a walking dream encased in a white coat. She had a pile of brown packets in her arms and he was at her side in an instant.

"Would you like a hand with those?" he inquired solicitously.

She smiled at him sweetly.

"Thank you, that would be very nice of you," she said, and then she saw Dave drinking contentedly and secretively and looked at him in amazement, her eyes wide open with surprise. "What have you got in your mouth?"

Dave took the tube out from between his lips. "A little light refreshment," he said innocently, "to help me through the morning."

"Are you going to give me a hand too?" she asked.

Dave tried to disentangle himself from his tube and nodded at her with a wide grin. When Helga asked for help, no boy in his right mind refused.

Meanwhile, down in the art room, Peter was busy with his preparations for the school dance. He was surrounded by rolls of curtains and decorations, each ready to be put up in the hall when the time came. At the moment he was sitting in a corner of the room working busily on a piece of glassware that bore a close resemblance to a pint tankard. He was performing a very delicate operation which consisted of removing the handle of the glass with a small blowlamp and then putting it back on again in a slightly different way so that if anyone picked it up when it was full and tried to drink out of it, the handle would snap off.

"It's really very ingenious," he said to himself when he had finished, and examined his handiwork with satisfaction. Then he put his masterpiece safely out of sight so that nobody could play about with it before it was needed.

The door of the art room opened and a girl from the fifth form came in. She was quite petite and strikingly pretty, with long brown hair and large hazel eyes. She made her way slowly around the room, pretending to look at the art exhibits on the walls and tables, and she kept glancing at Peter to see if he had noticed her but he had resumed work on the decorations for the school dance and was busy.

"Hello," she said at last, a little shyly, "I'm looking for Peter."

"He's not here," said Peter.

A puzzled look came over her face.

"But aren't you Peter?" she asked.

"Who wants to know?" he demanded.

"I do," she said.

"If you know I'm Peter, why did you say you were looking for him?"

The girl started to look confused and Peter began to feel sorry for her.

"What do you want?" he asked.

"I wondered if you needed any help," she said. "One of my friends told me you were looking for models."

He stopped work on a cardboard tube he was painting and studied her more closely. Then he stood up and slowly walked all around her. If nothing else, Peter was certainly in charge of his own small domain and he enjoyed every minute of it.

"What's your name?" he asked.

"Catherine," she replied a little self-consciously, aware that he was studying her very closely. "What sort of pictures do you paint?"

"Didn't your friend tell you?"

"Not exactly."

Peter noticed her hands. She had very long fingernails and they were painted red. He looked at them intently for a few moments and his eyes shone.

"Catherine," he said enthusiastically, "you're just what I've been looking for!"

"Am I?" she responded, not quite knowing why.

"Yes!" he said, and picked up one of his cardboard tubes. "I'm making this for the school dance. It's a pointing finger. Your fingernails are perfect. I'm going to copy them, and it'll be *your* finger that's pointing at everyone in the hall."

"Don't I have to take my clothes off?" asked Catherine in disappointment. "I thought models always had to undress."

Nobody believes this happens to me, thought Peter. It goes on all the time, and do any of my friends believe me?

Later that morning, Brian and Dave found Miles in the gymnasium after searching for him around the entire school. He was weightlifting, and had been working himself hard for the past hour. They hopped up onto a vaulting horse and watched in fascination.

"I'm getting into training," he explained, puffing and panting between each word. "Got to be fit and ready for when the time comes."

"Yes," said Brian doubtfully. "Good idea."

Miles turned his attention from the weights to a heavy punchbag hanging nearby. He hunched his shoulders and drove his fists into it with a succession of rapid punches. The bag sagged to one side with each thud.

"Why," asked Dave slowly, "have you got to be fit for when the time comes?"

"Very important," gasped Miles.

"*What* time?"

The punchbag continued to take a pummelling.

"The school dance," said Miles. "Got to be fit and ready for it. You just watch me! I reckon I'll be fit and ready for anything. Want a go?"

"At what?" asked Brian, "Suzanne?"

"At the punchbag!"

"No thanks," said Dave. "We've been carrying physics textbooks around the school all morning." He turned to Brian. "You and your big mouth. 'Oh,' this stupid idiot says to Helga, 'would you like a hand with those?' And the next thing I know we're lugging millions of the bastards all over the place."

"But did you see the way she smiled at me?" said Brian wistfully. "It was lovely. I don't think I'll ever forget the way she smiled at me. I'm in love with her."

Miles laughed. Then he gave the punchbag a final right hook and stepped back to wipe his hand across his forehead. He picked up his blazer from the floor and they left the gymnasium and began to wander slowly around the outside of the school buildings.

"Why did you laugh," asked Brian, "when I said I'm in love?"

"You'll need to take your place in the queue," said Miles, "and it's a long one. Haven't you noticed? Helga's got most of the boys in the sixth form tied up in knots, and a few of the teachers as well."

There was a sound of heavy running footsteps behind and Paul Brown assailed them. He, too, was keeping himself fit, by running around the school a hundred times, and when he caught up with them he asked Miles why nobody ever took him seriously. For a moment Miles wondered what he was talking about.

"What are you talking about?" asked Miles kindly.

"I don't think anybody takes me seriously," said Paul seriously. "If they did, then why do they keep running away from me?"

"Perhaps that's because they take you *too* seriously," said Miles carefully, afraid of unleashing one of Paul's fearful twitches by a carelessly-made remark. "Have you thought of that?"

"Drink?" offered Dave, producing the beer can from his

blazer pocket.

Paul stared at him and began to resume his run. "Are you serious?" he asked incredulously.

"He mightn't be, but I am," said Miles, reaching out for the can. "Thanks very much, Dave." He swirled the beer around in the can and swallowed it in one gulp. "Ah, that's better!" He handed the can back to Dave, who took it thinking that there was some left. When he discovered that it was empty, he glowered at Miles and threw the can to one side. It landed in a flowerbed.

Suddenly a window nearby opened and the headmaster's face appeared. His expression was a mixture of anger and disbelief.

"I saw you drop that can!" he said, looking as if he were about to have an apoplectic fit. "How dare you do that! Pick it up at once and get rid of it properly!"

"Oh, go and get stuffed, you stupid old fool," muttered Dave under his breath.

"Did you say something?"

"No sir, didn't say a thing, sir."

"Huh!" said Brian.

"Eh? What was that?"

Brian turned it into a loud spluttering sound as if he were clearing his throat. "Got a nasty cough, sir."

Dave picked up the can from the flowerbed.

"What would you like me to do with it, sir?"

"*I* don't know!" snapped the headmaster. "Put it with the rubbish." He went back in again and closed the window.

"Just as you say, sir," said Dave, and dropped it back on the earth border directly beneath the study window.

"Let's go for another ride in the car," said Brian. "It's your turn to take us, Dave. Where shall we go today?"

"I'll drive you around the school," said Dave.

"It's against the rules," said Miles piously.

"That's settled, then," said Brian. "Around the school we'll go."

So they waited for lunchtime when there would be a lot of

people about on the assumption that if there were a lot of people about nobody would pay much attention to them driving around in Dave's mother's Mini, and they set off on a tour of the school. While Dave sat hunched behind the steering wheel, Brian leaned out of the passenger window and Miles sat folded in half on the back seat. Brian whistled loudly every time they passed a girl who took his fancy.

"I can just imagine what *she* looks like without any clothes on," he bluffed boldly.

"Who?" asked Miles, twisting his head around from side to side, trying to peer out of the rear window whilst the car bumped along madly, but Brian wouldn't say any more, leaving him feeling disturbed and mystified. Dave was so disturbed and mystified that he decided not to drive around the school any longer and drove off down the drive towards the main road.

"Where are we going?" asked Brian, wondering why Dave had decided to abandon their tour of the school.

"I don't know," said Dave vaguely. They set off on a new expedition to the centre of Kingshampton, only this one had less of the dash and verve of Miles's drive in his father's powerful Rover and more the hopping and swerving of a startled rabbit, for Dave was none too precise with his steering and most of the time he was looking anywhere except where he was going. The ruts and potholes that had been treated contemptuously by the Rover proved more of a challenge to the ageing Mini, which skittered and slid all over the place and set Miles's teeth chattering uncontrollably in the back so that he was hardly able to utter a word.

Very soon they got into town and had a lot of fun trying to attract people's attention. They spotted Philip Rosser coming out of a fish and chip shop with a large bag of greasy fish and chips in his hands, and Dave swerved towards the pavement and gave a toot on the horn. Philip Rosser saw them coming at the last moment and leapt out of the way, scattering his fish and chips all over the road.

"Not my fault!" babbled Dave. "This car's got a mind of its

own!" And it dived into the nearest side street while Philip Rosser stood in the middle of the road bawling after them.

They passed the bus station and gave shouts and whistles to all the pretty girls in sight. Dave tangled briefly with a bus that got in his way, missed the front of it by inches and shot off in a new direction. It was head-whirling, eye-popping progress and Brian suspected that if it went on much longer he would end up in the driver's seat, with Miles upside-down next to him and Dave in the back. They were all thoroughly enjoying themselves.

"Let's go to the pub," suggested Dave. "I want a drink."

"You're not meant to drink and drive," pointed out Miles angelically.

"I wasn't intending to drink and drive," said Dave. "I was intending to drink first and then drive afterwards. Anyway, I had a drink earlier and it has made no difference to my driving whatsoever." He swerved to avoid a wall. "See? I missed that, didn't I?"

"I want to go back to school," said Brian suddenly, wondering if he should start praying.

"You're crazy," said Dave morosely, wrenching the steering wheel savagely in one direction.

"So do I," said Miles in fervent agreement with Brian.

"You're both crazy," said Dave even more morosely, wrenching the steering wheel savagely back again. "I don't care if you do want to go back to school."

"Let's go, then," said Brian. "I can just imagine what she looks like in bed." He had a faraway look in his eyes.

"Who's she?" demanded Dave suspiciously.

But Brian refused to say any more, and they began to feel disturbed and mystified all over again. It left Dave so disturbed and mystified that he decided not to drive around town any longer and drove back to school instead, hoping that the girl of Brian's imagination would appear before him like some wondrous apparition.

Chapter 10

Peter loved organising the school dance. Only members of the sixth form were allowed to go, together with anyone else they cared to take with them, and usually invitations were sent to the sixth forms of other schools in neighbouring towns, especially those that played against them in rugby, hockey and netball. It was held in the school assembly hall after Peter and his small team of helpers from the art room had spent the day putting up all the specially-prepared decorations. On this occasion his theme was anatomy, so the hall was festooned with pointing fingers, suspended ears, huge staring eyes with great eyelashes and large pairs of open lips drawn back over parted teeth. There were balloons everywhere, and the lighting was rigged up on tall stands to produce a blending of colours over the entire spectrum, ranging from reds, oranges and yellows to greens and blues with a touch of violet. Where the light beams met, there were vivid bursts and splashes of psychedelic colour that defied description. Large areas of shadow were left in the corners where all the low seats and tables from the sixth form common room had been placed. Long black curtains hung from the ceiling to produce an impressive background, with parts of the hall concealed to provide areas of privacy away from the dance-floor.

By half-past seven the evening had got well under way and heavy music was thudding out from four huge loudspeakers, making the hall vibrate with deafening songs, movement, shouting and laughter. The party atmosphere was filled with tobacco smoke mixed with the scent of a hundred perfumes and after-shave lotions. Everyone loved it. The hall was already full of people and more kept arriving all the time.

Brian had been standing outside in the lobby for some while, waiting for Miles and Dave to turn up. He was dressed in a flowery shirt with a huge necktie and a blue denim jacket, and his trousers flared out at the bottom and were so long that they would have rubbed against the ground if it were not for the fact that the boots on his feet raised his height by at least two inches, making him seem monstrous and ungainly. Although he liked to appear fashionable, he felt rather conspicuous, especially as he had washed his hair for the occasion and now it stuck out from his head like a frizzy mop. He had got there early so that he could watch all the girls arriving and see which one he fancied most. It was proving quite a revelation, for now that they were out of their school uniforms, anything seemed to go. Some of the skirts were the shortest he had ever seen, and most of the tops were cut so low that wherever he looked he got an eyeful of tit. He felt his head start to whirl with excitement.

Miles was the next to arrive, wearing an open-necked shirt, brown sports jacket and a pair of dark well-pressed trousers. There was something strangely conventional about his appearance that made him look like the head boy about to go out for the evening with his parents and the expression on his face was at its most angelic. He smiled beatifically at Brian.

"My ticket doesn't say anything about refreshments," he said, and whipped a bottle of whisky out of his pocket. "This is in case we get thirsty," he added, and put it back. Brian gaped at him, for one of the rules of the school dance stated that alcoholic drinks were not allowed anywhere near the hall. Members of staff would be there to make sure that everyone conducted themselves obediently and behaved well.

"If you get caught with that," said Brian in a hoarse whisper, "they'll confiscate it and throw you out."

"They've got to catch me first," replied Miles cunningly. "Ah, here comes Dave. Hello, who's this he's got with him?"

Dave sauntered into the lobby with a young woman on his arm who looked particularly gorgeous. He led her over towards Miles and Brian with a swagger in his step.

"Hello, boys," he said. "This is Jane."

Miles and Brian stared at her and exchanged awe-struck glances with each other.

"Hello," said Miles, recovering quickly. "Dave has told us a lot about you."

"Has he?" replied Jane. "So you must be Miles or Brian."

"I'm Miles," said Miles. "He's Brian."

Brian sidled up alongside her and goggled unashamedly at her with bulging eyes.

"Hello," he said, "I'm Brian."

"You're Brian?" she repeated, and gave a laugh.

"I suppose I am," sighed Brian. "Why are you laughing at me?"

Her laugh increased. "Because you've got fluffy hair."

"I suppose I have," agreed Brian, feeling downcast, and sidled off again.

Miles looked her up and down, enjoying the visual feast. So this was Jane, the apparent figment of Dave's imagination, the girl who worked in a small boutique in the centre of town. Well, she certainly knew how to make the best of herself. She was wearing an expensive red dress which looked as if it had just come out of the shop window and around her neck and wrist she wore a matching gold necklace and bracelet. She had an air of sophistication about her in the way she held herself and the manner in which she stood regarding them, and she made Miles feel uncomfortably out of his depth. "Shall we go in?" she said to Dave and he raced ahead to open the hall door for her. The four of them struggled past groups of young people, mostly with unfamiliar faces, clustered by the entrance and plunged headlong into the darkened depths of the hall.

Arnold immediately came up to them and stood swaying to

and fro. They seemed to swim about disconcertingly in front of his unsteady gaze.

"It's a wonderful dance, boys," he announced with an exaggerated pronunciation of the words, putting his hands out in front of him to keep his balance. "Get in there, it's really great."

"Yes, Arnold," said Miles, patting him on the shoulder like an old friend.

Jane peered at him in surprise.

"Has he been drinking?" she inquired.

Miles gave the matter his considered opinion.

"Oh no, it's not allowed," he said. "The school dance is always more sober than a temperance meeting. Besides, he's like this all the time, aren't you, Arnold? Arnold?"

Arnold had toppled over backwards and collapsed against the nearest curtains, which he clung to as tightly as he could. They picked him up again and set him on his feet until he recovered his equilibrium and tottered off. Brian gazed longingly towards the dance-floor where lots of pretty girls were dancing together.

"I want a girl..." he said suddenly, "...to have a dance with me."

Miles gestured towards the dance-floor.

"Take your pick," he said. "They all seem to be available. Look, there's one over there." He pointed to a beautiful young girl with long fair hair dancing on her own.

Brian rushed over to her.

"Hello, darling," he said dreamily. "How about a bit of sex?"

"Pardon?" said the girl, quite shocked.

"I meant how about a dance?"

"A dance? What's that got to do with sex?"

"It's only just the beginning," said Brian knowingly.

"Sauce!" squeaked the girl, and that was the last he saw of her.

Miles and Dave watched, and glanced at each other hopelessly.

"He made a right mess of that one," remarked Miles. "What's the matter?" he said when Brian returned, "didn't she want you?"

"It's always the same," grumbled Brian. "Nobody wants me."

Jane began dragging Dave towards the dance-floor.

"Maybe it's your hair," suggested Dave helpfully, calling back over his shoulder.

"What's wrong with my hair?" demanded Brian, turning to Miles, who had disappeared in search of Peter. Brian followed Miles over to the stage, where Peter was in charge of the record player and the lights, dressed up in a velvet jacket and big bow tie. When he wasn't changing records he was making all the lights go up and down and when he wasn't making all the lights go up and down he was changing records. When he wasn't changing records or making all the lights go up and down he was shouting into a microphone and when he wasn't doing any of these things he was drinking surreptitiously out of a glass which was supposed to have a soft drink in it but looked more like beer, for he had noticed that all of the supervising staff had got tired of the din and retired to a safe distance. When it looked as though any of them were thinking of coming back in, he turned the music up a bit more. The songs of Slade, Queen and T-Rex reverberated around the hall.

"Hello," said Peter, weaving slightly. "What are you blokes up to?"

"We've come to tell you how much we're enjoying the dance," answered Miles, and then clicked his tongue reproachfully. "Have you been at it already, like Arnold?"

"At what already?" asked Peter, blinking at them. "And who's Arnold?"

"At the booze, of course!"

"Certainly not!" Peter suddenly leaned over and lowered his voice. "Well, as a matter of fact, I'm trying to arrange a drinking contest." He winked at Miles and pointed in Dave's direction. Then he looked a bit harder and turned back to

Miles. "Who's that girl with Dave?"

"That," said Miles in a resigned voice, "is the famous Jane we thought didn't exist. Well, she does exist after all, as you can see."

"Bit of a good-looker, isn't she?" said Peter, impressed.

"She made fun of my hair," said Brian morosely.

"And she seems to have Dave running around in circles after her," added Miles, "so how about getting on with the contest?"

Peter grinned and nodded. He brought the music to a halt and grabbed the microphone.

"Ladies and gentlemen!" he called. "Can I have your attention, please? We're stopping the dance for a few moments to announce that in five minutes' time we're going to hold a special event." There were cheers and shouts from the floor. Peter held one hand up for silence. "We've decided we're going to have a drinking contest." There was more cheering and shouting. "Anybody who would like to take part, please make their way up to the stage." He caught Dave's attention and looked at him rather pointedly.

"Sounds like a good idea to me!" shouted back Dave from the dance-floor, and made his way through the crowd with Jane following closely behind.

"Who's taking part?" asked Peter into the microphone.

"Anyone who cares to take me on," suggested Dave boastfully, making a sweeping gesture with his hand.

"There's the challenge!" said Peter dramatically, and quickly bent down to pick something up off the floor. "I happen to have here a beer glass – what a bit of luck, eh? Because you'll need a glass if you're going to do it properly."

"Oh yes," said Dave, "it'll have to be done properly."

"I've never watched a drinking contest before," said Jane with mild curiosity.

Peter put on another record and turned up the volume even more in case any of the staff were tempted to come into the hall to find out why everything had suddenly gone quiet. Then, with the flourish of a professional conjurer about to perform a trick, he magically produced two cans of beer out of nowhere, opened them and began to fill the glass. There were loud cheers and a stamping of feet in approval.

Dave grinned at everybody and picked up the glass.

"Are you ready?" asked Peter and Dave nodded, smacking his lips in anticipation.

"Here goes!" he shouted, lifting the glass to his mouth. "Is anyone timing me?"

They were all watching in fascination. Suddenly, at the moment when it was meant to happen, there was a loud crack from the glass and without any warning it became detached from its handle. It fell to the ground and spilled its contents over him as it went. He was left standing gaping, still holding the handle. Everyone roared with laughter. The glass lay smashed at his feet, surrounding him in a large pool of beer.

"All right, who fixed the glass?" snarled Dave, turning to look for Peter. But Peter had mysteriously vanished.

So, too, had Miles. During the elaborate preparation of the drinking contest he had seen Suzanne sitting with another girl at one of the tables and took his chance to slip away quietly from the others. Only Brian noticed him go, and watched to see what happened next.

Miles casually went up to the two girls and sat down in a vacant seat beside Suzanne.

"Hello," he said, giving her his most ingenuous smile. ."What's a nice girl like you doing at an awful dance like this?"

Suzanne glanced at her friend and they both giggled.

"Perhaps I'm not really a nice girl," she said.

"Or perhaps this isn't such an awful dance either," he added. They both stared at each other seriously for a moment and then laughed.

"Are you trying to say you fancy me?" asked Suzanne.

"Do I look as though I am?" countered Miles innocently.

"Yes."

"All right, then, I fancy you."

The girl on the other side of Suzanne kept on giggling.

"What's wrong?" said Miles. "Do you mind me fancying your friend?"

"No, not at all," said the girl.

"And do you mind if I ask her if she'll have a dance with me?"

"No," said the girl.

Miles turned to Suzanne, who was finding it difficult to hide her amusement.

"Would you do me the great honour of having a dance?" he asked, standing up with an outstretched hand. She inclined her head with a smile, stood up as well and walked out to the dance-floor with him.

Brian was gaping at them with his mouth wide open. "Bloody hell," he muttered to himself, "so that's how he does it." A new, determined expression came over his face. He ran his hands over his hair to make sure it was all in the proper place, which was everywhere, and pushed his way through to the other girl, who was now sitting alone.

"Hello," he said, trying to put on the same sort of smile that Miles had done. "What's an awful girl like you doing at a nice dance like this? Oh hell! I mean—"

The girl stared at him.

"What did you say?"

"I'm sorry, I got that all wrong," said Brian. "What I meant to say was—"

The girl peered up at him.

"Do I know you?"

"No, but I don't half fancy you."

She giggled. "I'm sorry, but your friend has already beaten you to it," she said and waved to Peter, who was hiding behind the curtains nearby. Peter waved back.

"Everyone's against me," wailed Brian in despair. "It's a plot, that's what it is! It's a filthy plot! I know a filthy plot when I see one!"

Miles and Suzanne had their dance together and afterwards, instead of returning to join her friend, she let Miles take hold of her hand. He whispered something in her ear and they began to make their way across the hall towards the lobby. They picked their way through the thronging masses of young people, who were getting noisier and more exuberant with every passing minute, and finally emerged into the quiet dimness of the school vestibule where the sounds of the dance were reduced to a dull, low thudding.

They stopped in the middle of the lobby and breathed in the cool air. Miles looked around at the trophy cabinets, the framed photographs of the rugby team, the rolls of honour inscribed with the names of head boys and head girls. It was all so familiar to him for he had walked through there several times each day for the last seven years, but now it was different. Now it had an intimacy that he could not describe. He turned his attention back to Suzanne. She was looking at him expectantly.

For a moment he studied her in the half-light, from her pretty face with its bright blue eyes and long flowing blonde hair to the figure displayed beneath her party dress. This was no longer the girl he had seen in the library in school uniform, her bag slung casually over one arm. This was a slender and beautiful young woman, full of breathtaking femininity.

"Why don't we walk around the school?" he said at last. "It's quiet, and nobody will disturb us. We can talk then."

She looked up at him and smiled, and he reached out for her and put his arm around her shoulder. He felt her own hand pressing against his waist.

"What shall we talk about?"

He shrugged slightly. "Anything you like. Why did you come to the dance tonight?"

She glanced at him as though she couldn't understand why he had asked. "I like dances. Sometimes I go to the disco in town. It's fun."

"I came because—" He paused for a moment, thinking of saying "—because I thought you might be here," but it seemed such an obvious thing to say. She looked at him with large inquiring eyes that made his heart beat faster, and he knew he had to say it. "I came because I hoped I'd see you here."

She smiled.

"I hoped to see you, too," she said softly, and suddenly everything seemed to be all right. He squeezed her shoulder and felt her respond with a tighter hold of her own. They left the lobby and walked into one of the quadrangles, passing the school noticeboard where there was a large poster for the school dance pinned up. It was one of Peter's finer efforts. Miles took it down and carried it along with him.

"There's a group of you," said Suzanne, "and you're all in second year science, aren't you?"

"That's right," he grinned. "And all of us are completely dedicated to the cause."

"What cause?"

"The cause of not doing any work."

She looked at him again, this time with a puzzled and uncertain expression.

"I tell you what," said Miles, "let's go up to the common room and I'll explain everything about it. I hear they've got the coffee machine working properly for once, so we can have something to drink."

"Won't the common room be locked?"

"I don't know. Let's go and find out."

They went up the long flight of steps to the balcony and walked along it in darkness until they came to the common room door. Miles tried the handle and the door opened. They went in and switched the lights on. Miles placed the poster down on the window-sill and went over to the coffee machine. He put some coins in it and got two beakers of steaming hot drinking chocolate. He gave one to Suzanne and they went to sit down by the window. He took the whisky bottle from his pocket and poured some into his chocolate. He offered the bottle to her but she shook her head. They both had a few sips and regarded each other over the tops of their beakers.

"You said you were going to tell me all about it," said

Suzanne. "About the cause, I mean. Don't you do any work at all?"

"Well, that depends," said Miles, considering the question. "Sometimes when we feel like it we go to the occasional lesson, but mostly we don't feel like it so we don't go. It's as simple as that."

"But doesn't anyone mind? Don't they say anything?"

"Oh no. They don't say anything because they don't mind. Or they don't mind so they don't say anything. School is about the biggest contradiction that has ever existed. What does it do except teach you how to realise that education is supposed to be something big and wonderful that never finishes and all the time you've forgotten where it started. It's like going on a very long journey and not being able to remember where it began or know where it's going to end. You're just in the middle of something so large that you don't know where you are with it."

"That sounds like quite a philosophy."

"It is. I don't simply accept everything like the rest of you in this awful place. I question it when I think it needs questioning."

"But where does it get you in the end?"

"It gives me a good excuse for not doing any work," said Miles with a grin.

"Seriously."

"I *am* being serious."

"So is that what you do in the library? Nothing?"

He nodded. "Yes, most of the time. Sometimes I think about how I would rid the school of the headmaster. And then I think it would be better not to get rid of him at all. I'd get rid of the deputy instead, because he's a nuisance, and then with the deputy gone the school would fall apart so they'd have to remove the headmaster as well and find someone else to put in his place. Another one I can't stand the sight of is my maths master. Do you take maths?"

Suzanne shook her head.

"You don't realise how lucky you are," said Miles. "He has

the most unfortunate effect on me. There again, I'm not sure if it's the master or the subject, but Dave doesn't like him much either and he doesn't even take maths any more."

"Who's Dave?"

"My friend who got himself drowned in beer earlier." Then Miles told her what they had done to Smith the other day and how maths had been to blame for that.

Suzanne gave him a sideways look. "I don't think you like anyone at school," she said at last.

"One exception."

"Who?"

"Who do you think?"

They both laughed.

"Do you mean that?"

"Of course I do!"

"Go on, then – prove it. Show me how much," she giggled, and Miles gave her a kiss on one cheek. She pulled him closer. "That's not the way to do it," she said, and kissed him on the lips.

It was some time later when he picked up the poster that he had left on the window-sill and, thinking carefully for a few minutes, he made up several lines of verse which he wrote down on the back. This is how it went:

What is life but a flowing river
In which I am but an atom of existence.
It matters not what I do
For everything must end
So why not make a gesture of resistance?

And at the bottom he wrote "Ode from M. to S."

"You're a poet, Miles," said Suzanne in delight.

"No I'm not," he said. "It's true." He clapped his hands together. "And now I'll show you something I made up the other day in the library during a particularly idle moment." He picked up the poster again and wrote the following limerick:

There was an old man called the Head
Who liked to see young girls in bed
And although he was lazy
The sight sent him crazy
Until one day he dropped down dead.

"The first one is for you," said Miles and carefully tore it off to give to her. Then he took the poster back down to the noticeboard and pinned it up again.

Chapter 11

Miles carefully planned the timing of his next arrival in school for when all the fuss had died down over the appearance of the poster with its little appendage, only to find that it had not died down at all.

The headmaster was having a fit in his study.

"Insolence!" he roared at the secretary. "Sheer insolence! How does anyone *dare* to do such a thing? I mean, it's not even *true!*"

"No, of course it's not," said the secretary in a consoling voice, wondering.

The headmaster wished that it were true when he thought about some of his staff, but he didn't say so.

"I think I shall just ignore it," he said majestically. "If I just ignore it, it will soon be forgotten. And if it's *not* soon forgotten, I think I shall just ignore it anyway."

"What happens if you ignore it but it's never forgotten?" inquired the secretary with the greatest of delicacy.

"Then I shall be all the more pleased that I ignored it," said the headmaster with devastating logic. He made up his mind never to take assembly again, ever. In fact, he made up his mind never to poke his head outside his study door without firstly making sure that the lobby was empty. Instead, he sat in his study like an unlikely ruler, hidden away from the harsh reality and brazen rudeness of a school which regarded him as the personification of a retreating general who was near to the point where he could no longer stand the strain of his own disastrous making and was about to turn and run. Except that the headmaster had not the slightest intention of running. He was too solidly entrenched in his own grievous misfortune, forever complaining of his duties whilst manifestly failing to carry them out.

Miles heard all about it from Francesca, who heard all about it from the secretary when she wasn't hearing all about it through the open door between the study and the office.

"I can just imagine his face," she said, "when he first read it."

"Read what?" asked Miles innocently.

"Haven't you heard?" she said breathlessly. "Somebody wrote a rude poem about him and left it on the school noticeboard."

"How awful," said Miles. "What was his face like when you imagined it?"

"Indescribable," said Francesca.

"Not much different from usual, then," said Miles.

"Only indescribably worse," she added.

"I wonder if it's true, what it said about him."

"How do you know what it said?" asked Francesca in surprise.

"Word gets around," said Miles airily. "Do you know what it said?"

"Oh no," said Francesca. "Nobody's supposed to know. The secretary tore it up at once. She put all the bits in different bins so nobody could piece them together again afterwards. I can just imagine what her face was like when she read it."

"It sounds a very interesting poem," said Miles and crept out of the office in case the headmaster heard him and demanded to know who it was creeping out of the office. He crept up to the library, where he found Suzanne doing some work. Since she was the only person, apart from himself, who knew that he was responsible for writing the verse, he got her to promise not to tell anyone.

"What would you do if I did?" she asked in a teasing voice

when he got her in a quiet corner to give her a kiss while nobody was looking.

"That depends," he said. "What would you do if I told everyone that we went to bed together last night?"

She blinked in astonishment.

"But we didn't go to bed together last night," she pointed out.

"So you promise not to tell anyone?" he persisted.

"Yes," she said, slightly confused, and went off to her next lesson.

Miles spent the rest of the morning with his head in a textbook, not reading a word of it. Brian and Dave didn't know that he wasn't reading a word of it and they wondered if he was feeling ill all of a sudden.

"Are you feeling all right?" asked Brian diplomatically.

"No," said Miles.

They exchanged knowing glances behind his back.

"What do you want to know for?" he demanded without looking up from his book.

"We were just wondering," said Dave, "how did you get on with Suzanne at the dance?"

"Not bad," said Miles.

"That's good," said Brian.

"We were also wondering," said Dave, "how did you get on with Suzanne *after* the dance?"

"Not bad," said Miles.

"That's good," said Brian.

Miles looked at them both in mild exasperation. "What's the matter with you two idiots this morning?" he asked.

"Nothing," said Dave. "She looks a very nice girl."

"She is," said Miles.

"That's good," said Brian, "but we think you ought to put your book away, all the same. You know what they say about girls and books – they don't mix."

The main obstacle they had to overcome was physics. If they went to physics, no one noticed they were there, but if they didn't go to physics, they feared that their absence would immediately be remarked upon and questions might be asked. As a matter of fact, neither their presence in physics nor their absence from it was ever met with anything other than indifference and disregard.

On the supposition that they were not in a position to know much about it either way, they came to the conclusion that it wouldn't do any harm to go along and put in the occasional appearance provided it didn't involve any work. And they knew it was quite safe to go to physics because no one would notice that they were there, and this might give them a chance to find out if their absence on other days was remarked upon and whether questions were being asked.

Miles decided to find out from John. John knew a great deal about physics because he liked it and worked very hard at it and talked to lots of other people about it. Lots of other people avoided him whenever possible because they didn't like being talked to about it, but Miles didn't mind talking about it because it gave him an opportunity to show how much he didn't know.

So they went along to physics and sat next to John, who was being scrupulously avoided by everyone else.

"Do you know what the speed of light has to do with energy?" John asked them in a low voice.

"No, not particularly," answered Miles.

"I shan't tell you, then," said John in a huff. "Do you want to know why pressure affects boiling?"

"Can't say I do," replied Miles. "Do you want to know why you get on my tit?"

John grinned.

"You're crazy, all three of you. You're like Mad Mike over there. He's crazy, too."

Mad Mike often discussed physics with John because John knew a lot about physics and Mad Mike didn't, and Mad Mike knew he had to get the top grade in his physics A-level otherwise he wouldn't get a place in university. Mad Mike was known to be particularly adept at wiring up circuits wrongly during practical lessons and then burning out the highly-sensitive and expensive voltmeters. He used to enjoy watching the wires smoking.

Paul Brown wanted to take physics but they wouldn't let him. They told him he wouldn't understand how hard it was, which didn't convince him because he really *didn't* understand how hard it was and probably never would. He consulted Miles on the matter.

"Physics *is* hard," Miles assured him. "Don't be under any illusion, it's *very* hard."

"But how do you know?" wailed Paul.

"Well, I don't," admitted Miles quietly, "but they tell me it is. Anyway, I fully expect to fail it."

"Anyone can fail it," scoffed Paul. "I want some advice from someone who's going to pass."

"You want some advice from a psychiatrist," advised Miles sententiously.

So Paul Brown didn't take physics, which was a great relief to all those who did, including Miles, who was Paul's best friend. Paul had very few friends, mainly because of his twitch, and Miles kept feeling rather sorry for him.

The physics master was Mr Bates. He had a clean fresh face and wavy auburn hair just starting to turn grey. He wore a pair of tortoise-shell spectacles and always dressed in a smart tweed sports jacket. He was brisk, efficient and very good. Most people didn't like him because he used to wear them out with copious notes and enjoyed frightening physics into them with an almost unceasing, explosive energy. His tireless efforts were rewarded with excellent examination results. Miles, Brian and Dave had tried asking for a transfer to another group, but the request was either ignored or disregarded, leaving them defenceless in the face of Mr Bates's terrific onslaught.

They did the only thing that seemed reasonable – miss lessons whenever they could and go only when they dared, which was as rarely as possible.

"I don't know why I ever wanted to take physics," moaned Miles, feeling sorry for himself. "I should have taken something else, like R.E.," he added in a saintly voice.

"Do you know what I think of R.E.?" asked John.

Miles put his hands together and turned away. "I don't want to know what you think of *anything*," he said.

Soon John captured Mr Bates in a long discussion about what the speed of light had to do with energy, which was overheard by Mad Mike, who immediately asked Miles if he knew what they were talking about.

"I haven't the haziest notion about any of it," said Miles nonchalantly.

"Do you know anything at all about physics?" demanded Mad Mike.

"I know enough to fail it," answered Miles brightly.

"But do you think I know enough to pass it?" persisted Mad Mike. "I've *got* to pass or I'll never get to university."

"Hard luck," said Miles sympathetically. "I don't think you'll ever get to university. Why don't you try to fail it instead? It's far easier."

"But what's the good of that?" screamed Mad Mike. "I don't want to fail! I want to pass!"

"All right," said Miles. "What's the specific heat capacity of copper?"

"I don't know," moaned Mad Mike. "I'm done for. Can't you see I'm done for?"

"So am I," said Miles cheerfully. He pointed to Brian. "So is he." He pointed to Dave as well. "And him. We're all done for."

Brian and Dave both grinned and nodded.

"Are you?" asked Mad Mike faintly. "Truthfully?"

"Physics is merely a state of mind," elucidated Miles. "Either you love it or you hate it. Either you find it easy or you find it hard. Either you can do it or you can't. Agreed?"

"I suppose so," said Mad Mike, nodding miserably. "I hate it."

"That's a symptom of finding it hard."

"I find it hard."

"That's a symptom of wanting to give it up gracefully."

"I want to give it up gracefully. No I don't! Oh, what am I saying? I must be out of my mind!"

"What do you want to study at university?" asked Miles, trying a new approach.

"I don't even want to go to university any more," said Mad Mike. "It's my mother who wants me to go."

"Let me help you with some advice," offered Miles kindly. "Give up."

Mad Mike shook his head furiously and banged his fist down hard on the table. "No, no, I won't give up!" he protested.

After he had gone back to his place and Mr Bates had broken off his discussion with John, who was preparing to argue about optical path differences and interference, they got on with the lesson. It lasted for more than half of the morning, and Miles soon fell into a trance. His physical being remained sitting at the laboratory bench with books and files in front of him, but his mind was elsewhere. He was with Suzanne and they were running hand in hand through woods and meadows, crossing streams, joyful in each other's company. Their world was full of sunshine and laughter. He pictured them both in a gipsy caravan, travelling the lanes and by-ways. He saw her dressed in a simple peasant's costume with a long flowing skirt and a pink cotton smock. He felt her hair blowing against his face, he felt the warm, passionate kiss of her lips against his own.

It was, without doubt, the most pleasurable physics lesson he had been to for a long time.

Chapter 12

Mad Mike knew only too well when he was done for. Every day he got to school early, took his bag upstairs to the physics laboratory, which was his form room, and dumped it on the floor outside the door and then went looking for his friends, who mostly hung around in the assembly hall and talked until the bell went, when they made their way up to the lab for registration, which Miles always missed. Mad Mike was rarely absent and he got on well with all the staff because he was very polite and willing to work hard. He wanted to go to university to study engineering, but he knew it was only a forlorn hope. Not like Chris, his friend who had no chin but possessed a marvellously retentive memory which could effortlessly store up all the facts and methods. Nobody knew better than Mad Mike when he was done for, and he had known it ever since his mother wanted him to go to university to study engineering so that he could build roads and bridges and dams all over the world.

Mad Mike lived with his parents and sister, and walked to school every day. His home was on the opposite side of Kingshampton but he dutifully set off at quarter-past eight each morning and always got there with ten minutes to spare. He was a slightly dull and uninspiring sort of boy who lived his life according to timetables and regulations, but most people seemed to like him. He knew that he would probably grow up to become a dependable plodder, like his uncle who had a good job with the local council. Mad Mike could not imagine himself as a globe-trotting engineer.

He usually had his dinner in the canteen with Dave, and sometimes Bobbie joined them. Mad Mike envied Bobbie for taking geology instead of mathematics because she was always going on field-trips. He liked Bobbie, although he could not bring himself to show it too obviously. Harris followed Bobbie around the school like a pet poodle and made Mad Mike jealous.

Harris struggled through the queue which trailed away from the serving hatches and set his tray down noisily on the table next to Bobbie who was languidly prodding her fork into a piece of meat pie.

"Oh, bog off, Harris," grumbled Mad Mike. But Harris grinned at him and sat down beside Bobbie, who had her hair tied in plaits. He fingered one of the plaits, but Bobbie ignored him.

"This meat pie tastes awful," she said, forking another small morsel into her mouth.

"I'm not surprised," said Dave. "They've made it from yesterday's left-overs. Look, you can tell, it's got chopped up carrot in it and what vegetable did we have yesterday? Carrots."

Bobbie made a face at him.

Harris heaved himself energetically into his dinner and started cramming it into his mouth as fast as he could.

"It's all right," he said, although they found it hard to understand the words. "I like a bit of meat pie."

Dave pushed his own plate to one side in disgust and began poking at a dish of prunes and custard with a bent spoon. The custard had a thick yellow skin on it and he spent some time carefully peeling it off. The staff occupied a large table at the far end of the canteen and Dave always kept his head down low so that none of them would see him.

"Harris, have you just dropped one?" he demanded, wrinkling up his nose and staring across the table with a sour look on his face.

Bobbie sniggered and Harris couldn't pretend to evade the

question.

"Why?" he asked in a pause between mouthfuls.

"Just wondered," shrugged Dave casually, and Harris was momentarily thrown into a state of confusion. He often tried to break wind in morning assembly to make all his friends laugh, but one day the deputy caught him letting rip and sent him outside in disgrace, and he could be heard exploding in the lobby while everyone was singing the hymn, *Bless'd Are The Pure In Heart*.

Bobbie disliked him intensely as much as she liked Mad Mike for being so cute and gentle, and she hoped that Mad Mike would ask her out one night but he never did because he was too shy. She decided that she would just have to ask *him* out instead, but she didn't really want to in case it made him feel embarrassed.

"Why do you want me to take you out one night?" asked Mad Mike curiously. "Is it because you feel sorry for me?"

"I don't feel sorry for you," said Bobbie.

"That's the trouble," said Mad Mike miserably. "Nobody feels sorry for me, but they *ought* to."

"Take me out one night," hinted Bobbie kindly, "and I might do."

Harris wolfed his dinner down at such a speed that he had finished it all, including his pudding, whilst Dave was still delicately dissecting the last of his prunes and thinking about going down to the pub for a beer. Harris got up clumsily from the table, making all the plates and dishes rattle, gave Bobbie's hair another affectionate tweak and headed for the door, taking his own empty plates with him, which he handed through the end hatch to the dinner ladies in the kitchen. Once he was outside, they heard him belching loudly.

"No manners at all," said Dave self-righteously, shaking his head.

Mad Mike knew he was done for the moment he started taking A-level physics. He used to like it at one time when he regularly got at least seventy per cent in the class exams in the days when the staff took over a week to mark the papers towards the end of the summer term and let everyone in the school lie out on the field watching games of cricket and playing pocket-chess; but now he hated it. Instead, they threw nasty practicals at him and got him to set up Wheatstone Bridges just so that he could connect all the electrical apparatus wrongly together and burn out the expensive meters which sent howls of anguish through Mr Bates, although Helga always remained deliciously cool and unperturbed. Mad Mike got so frustrated by it that he often felt like crying.

"Will somebody help me?" he used to call out plaintively, and one day Miles went over to see if he could lend a hand. Of course, he had no more idea of what he was doing than Mad Mike did, but it gave him a chance to mess around without directly taking the blame. Since then, Mad Mike had regarded Miles as his best friend and offered all sorts of useless excuses to explain Miles's absence from applied maths.

Actually, Mad Mike had as much of a problem with applied maths as he did with physics, and nobody realised the problem more than Adrian, who was very good at mathematics. Mad Mike found Adrian in the library, where he usually spent most of his spare time if he wasn't to be found in the common room cuddling Honey, who persistently wouldn't wear a bra beneath her thin shirt so that Adrian could touch her fondly while everyone else was busy playing cards.

"Adrian," said Mad Mike, tapping him on the head with a pencil, "tell me how you figure out the Tangent Rule."

"By figuring out the Cosine Rule first," answered Adrian.

"How do you figure out the Cosine Rule?" asked Mad Mike hopelessly.

"It's ridiculously easy," said Adrian. "Why do you want to know?"

"Because I've got to pass," said Mad Mike desperately. "I've got to *pass*."

"How do you reckon that figuring out the Tangent Rule is going to help you?"

"Hasn't it helped *you?*"

"I don't know," said Adrian smugly. "I've never not known it."

Mad Mike looked at him dubiously, not sure whether he might be bluffing. Adrian had the sort of mind that dealt easily with mathematical logic and he was also a very good rugby player. The headmaster was only too delighted to shake him warmly by the hand every time he saw him and inquire if he was enjoying his latest cap.

"That boy is going to go far on the rugby field," predicted the headmaster proudly one day, and a week later Adrian was carried off with a broken leg and taken to hospital where he was bound up in plaster and bandages and sent back to school two days later on crutches.

"Good," said Mad Mike maliciously, thinking about Adrian's superior mathematical knowledge.

"Good," agreed Miles, thinking about Honey and how much he fancied her.

"It hurts," complained Adrian, "it hurts."

"A pity it wasn't Harris who got the broken leg," muttered Mad Mike darkly, watching Bobbie and wondering if he could ever summon up the courage to ask her out.

"Don't you like Harris?" asked Miles.

"No," said Mad Mike. "He wants to take Bobbie away from me. Can you imagine anything so sly and treacherous?"

"Doesn't anyone feel sorry for me?" asked Adrian in a pathetic voice, wobbling about on his crutches. Nobody did.

But Miles felt sorry for Bobbie because Mad Mike obviously didn't know what to do with her. He hadn't got a clue. He was helpless with girls, although Bobbie did all she could to interest him and arouse his natural instincts. She wore dark tights under her socks and put on a very short grey pleated skirt, and she tied up her long fair hair leaving two curling lovelocks. In her efforts to arouse Mad Mike's natural instincts, she only succeeded in arousing the natural instincts of others.

The deputy was hardly a young man, but he didn't let it pass unnoticed. He went to find the headmaster, who never took much searching for. He was testing the lock on his study door.

"I think it's grossly indecent," said the deputy, "a young girl flaunting herself around the school like that."

"Like what?" inquired the headmaster, suddenly becoming interested in doing some exploring.

The deputy gestured loosely and uselessly.

"Well how can I put it?" he said. "Showing her legs…and up here…"

The headmaster went to see for himself and viewed her across the library under the pretext of going to visit the librarian in her small room at the back. He suddenly became engrossed in searching through all of the bookshelves for a volume which the library did not seem to possess. Then he went back to his study and took his temperature, and when the secretary saw him she was so alarmed by his appearance that she sent for the school nurse, who took his blood pressure. The nurse was so astonished by it that she sent him home to have a rest. He stayed there for several days suffering from nervous prostration.

Chapter 13

One morning there was a sudden uproar in the office. Francesca was having an argument with the secretary. It went on for at least a minute, with raised voices, one or two squeals and shrieks, the sound of objects being thrown and then, just as quickly as it had started, the fuss died down and the office door was flung open. Francesca appeared.

"You're a useless little bitch!" screamed the secretary from behind her desk. "Do you hear me? You're an insolent little bitch as well!"

"And you're a horrible old bag!" screamed back Francesca. Out she came, stamping her feet in anger, and slammed the office door shut behind her with a tremendous crash. She stood where she was for a moment, dancing up and down with rage, and finally she burst into tears. She failed to observe Miles, Brian and Dave, who were walking through the vestibule on their way down to the pub and had now come to a standstill, staring at her in disbelief. She didn't notice them watching her but dried her eyes with a small paper tissue and then turned around and marched straight out of the school.

They looked at the office, then they looked at the disappearing figure of Francesca and lastly they looked at each other.

"Well," said Miles in a tone of mild bemusement, "I don't know what you two fellows have to say about it, but I think they've just had a row."

Dave looked at him in surprise. "Whatever gives you that idea?"

Miles hunched his shoulders aimlessly. "Oh, I suppose the use of words like 'bitch' and 'bag' gave me that impression. Let's go and find out."

They hurried after Francesca and caught up with her outside the school.

"Hello, where are you off to?" called out Miles cheerfully, pretending not to know that anything was wrong.

"Anywhere," she sniffed. "Anywhere away from here."

"Can't say I blame you," said Brian, and she stopped and turned to them. Her eyes were red and filled with moisture. She gave them another dab with her tissue.

"Do you know what that nasty old bat in the office just called me?" she said. "I bet you'll never guess!"

"She called you a useless little bitch," said Dave helpfully.

"Oh. How do you know?"

"Because we heard it," said Miles. "I wouldn't be surprised if half the school didn't hear it as well."

"Is that why you came after me?"

"Yes."

A smile gradually broke through her tear-stained face, like the sun coming out from behind the clouds. "That was nice of you." She sniffed again.

"As a matter of fact we were just on our way down to the pub," said Miles. "Would you like to join us? As a special concession, we promise not to regard you as a member of staff."

"The *pub?*" she said in surprise.

"That's right."

She gave a little laugh. "I'd love to." Then she paused. "But shouldn't you all be working, or something?"

"Oh, we will be," Miles assured her, and Brian and Dave nodded eagerly. "Wait here."

He ran back into the school grounds and reappeared a few moments later at the wheel of his father's white Rover. He pulled up alongside the pavement and leaned across to open

111

the passenger door for her. Francesca got into the front seat beside him and Brian and Dave jumped in the back. They roared off into the morning traffic and made their way down to the pub that they had been intending to visit. Within five minutes of leaving the school, they were settled into a dark corner and Francesca suddenly wondered if she knew what she was doing.

Miles carried four glasses over from the bar and put them down on the table. He passed Francesca the orange juice she had asked for and sat down next to her with his own pint of strong brew. Brian and Dave sat in the other two seats, clutching their glasses and looking remarkably self-conscious.

"I don't know if I can ever face going back after what happened this morning," said Francesca, breaking the silence. "For weeks that horrible old cow has been getting at me all the time – I know she doesn't like me. In fact, she can't stand the sight of me."

"Why doesn't she like you?" asked Miles in surprise. "I mean, *we* all like you, don't we?" He turned to Brian and Dave, and they nodded their heads vigorously.

"It's perfectly simple," said Francesca. "She doesn't like me for the same reason that you three do – because I'm young. To have me around the place every day makes her feel as she looks: old and shrivelled up. For her, the only consolation is that she can boss me about and know that she's perfectly entitled to do so and that if I so much as raise one finger in dissent she'd be justified in getting rid of me, which is what she wants to do anyway. I'm sure of that. And I can't tell you how much I'd love to go, I really would. But the last thing I want to do is give her the satisfaction."

They agreed they didn't like the secretary very much themselves.

"What does she do?" asked Brian.

"She's always making nasty remarks about me, usually to members of staff when they come into the office. I can't type properly. I can't spell properly. I can't see to the registers properly. I can't do *anything* properly, if you listen to her. And they *do* listen to her, that's the awful bit about it!'"

Her voice was beginning to sound querulous and she was working herself up to start crying again. Brian and Dave exchanged glances and pulled faces at each other. They each took a swig of beer.

"What happened this morning to cause the row?" asked Miles.

"She said I wasn't dressed properly. 'Oh, my dear,' she says – *'my dear'*, mind you – 'you can't possibly keep wearing those jeans and that jersey all the time. They look so untidy.' But why should she worry? It's how I've always dressed. She said the deputy headmaster wanted to see me looking more presentable. If the girls in the sixth form could do it, so could I, or something like that. I told her I'm not a girl in the sixth form and that I was going to wear what *I* wanted to wear and they couldn't stop me. When she said she'd soon see about that, I called her an interfering old bitch and that was how it started. It sort of went on from there and we just kept throwing insults at each other until I couldn't stand it any longer and that's when I left. I suppose I was in the wrong because I lost my temper, but I couldn't help it." She giggled. "Mind you, I did call her some terrible names."

"Did you?"

"Yes, I did. Well, she asked for it and as far as I'm concerned she got it! If I never see the inside of that place again I wouldn't care!"

"Same here," agreed Dave. The conversation paused and they all stared at the table. He picked up his glass and raised it to his mouth, tipped it back and drank its contents down in one go. "That's better," he said with a satisfied smirk on his face and put the empty glass back down on the table with a thud. He had done it at last in front of his two friends and they hadn't been able to stop him.

"You can buy your own drink in future," said Miles, pretending to look suitably taken aback.

Dave belched loudly.

"Pig," they said, even more shocked, and Francesca giggled

again in delight.

"Oh, you are funny, all of you," she said, and by now she was back to her usual bright self. Once again Miles caught a fleeting glimpse of her big dark eyes staring curiously at him, only to look away quickly at something else.

"Mind you," he said hastily, "*I* can't see anything wrong with the way you look." He leaned to one side and peered under the table where he could see the trouser legs of her jeans and a pair of dainty little red high-heeled shoes. He patted her on one knee. "I wish everyone in school looked like you. I might feel more like going then."

She inclined her head demurely and gave him a little smile of gratitude.

"Thank you," she said quietly. "You've been very kind and generous to me this morning. I don't know what I would have done if I hadn't had you to talk to." She sighed and gave a resigned shrug. "Well, I suppose I ought to go back now, say how sorry I am and see if it's accepted."

"Do you think it will be?"

"I hope so. Oh, I know I said how much I'd like to leave, but when I do go I want it to be of my own accord and not like this."

Miles stood up. "I'll run you back in the car," he said and turned to Brian and Dave. "You two may as well stay here, it's nearly lunchtime. Have one for me as well." He stepped aside for Francesca to come out of her corner. "Shall we go?"

Brian and Dave sat watching Miles and Francesca disappear out of the door. Brian was open-mouthed.

"Do you get the feeling we've just been out-manoeuvred?" he said incredulously.

"I don't know and I don't care," said Dave, picking up his empty glass. "You heard what the man said. He said 'have one for me as well' and that's exactly what I'm going to do."

Miles drove Francesca back to school and waited for her in the lobby while she went to make her peace with the secretary in the office, and a few minutes later she reappeared, looking more cheerful.

"Better now?" asked Miles and she nodded.

"Yes, thanks."

"Was your apology accepted?"

She nodded again.

"Yes, but not very graciously. Still, I didn't think it would be."

The lunchtime bell rang throughout the school and classroom doors began to open along the corridors.

"Dinnertime," said Miles brightly. "Are you feeling hungry?"

"Yes, I am a bit," said Francesca. Usually she took a packet of crisps and an apple in her bag and ate them in the office after the secretary had gone home, but Miles guessed correctly that she did not feel like staying in the office today, even though it was empty.

"In that case come with me," he said, and drove her back into Kingshampton again. They parked in one of the side streets and walked to the small bus station café.

"Before you say anything," said Francesca, "I'm buying lunch."

She ordered sandwiches and cups of tea and they took them over to a tiny table by the window. Miles watched her as they both ate and found himself admiring her in a way he had never done before. He didn't see who was crouching behind a discarded newspaper at another table on the far side of the room, he was too intently studying the minutest details of Francesca's face, the shape of her nose, the fine dark lines of her eyebrows, the movement of her lips. Until now she had been nothing more than the secretary's secretary, the lovely kind warm-hearted girl who conspired with Miles in his daily lateness but nevertheless remained one of the school's fixtures; now she was a living and pulsating soul who had come into his life by crossing over the dividing line which separated school from his own self, for now it felt that she belonged to him, at least for the present moment.

She spent a long time stirring her cup of tea and his gaze moved down to her fingers. He looked at the small dark hairs and the red nail varnish. She's got nice little hands, he thought, and then suddenly he was aware that she was speaking. "Do you know what you've done today, Miles?" she said. "You've made me feel that there is someone on my side after all. It's very important for me to know that, and to think that I've got at least one friend in school who cares about me."

He could see that she must have felt very lonely. It seemed strange for her to regard him as a friend, considering their previous relationship from school, she being a less important member of staff, he being a less important pupil, and now here they were sitting together in a café. Perhaps that was the reason why, but it felt uncomfortably surreal and Miles was no longer sure of himself, and that began to make him feel uneasy.

"Ho ho!" said the discarded newspaper suddenly, and Miles shot up. He raced over and tore the newspaper away from its amused reader, and Peter was sitting behind it. "Hello," he said with a big smile. "Having fun?"

Francesca laughed and stood up.

"Come on," she said to Miles, "I think we've been out of school for long enough."

Chapter 14

Brian and Dave were sitting in the library, contemplating school life. They had nothing else to do. Miles had not appeared yet that morning and they were rather puzzled by his unexplained absence.

"I hear they're thinking of closing the common room," said Brian at last, poking Dave to keep him awake.

"Are they?" said Dave, stirring himself. "What do they want to do that for?"

"Nobody seems to know. It's too bad. I won't be able to eat my lunch in there any more if it closes."

"I have *my* dinner in the canteen," said Dave smugly, "so it won't affect me."

"Miles won't like it either."

"Where is he, do you think?"

"I've no idea. But do you know something? I tried to ring him last night and there was no reply."

"Maybe he was out."

"He hardly ever goes out in the week."

Dave shrugged. "What were you ringing him for?"

"Oh, nothing particularly."

"Liar," said Dave. "You were still wondering what he was getting up to with Francesca."

"The thought did cross my mind," admitted Brian, "but only because..."

One of the prefects sitting at a nearby table looked over at them in irritation.

"Can't you two shut up? Some of us are trying to work in here."

Dave looked up and turned around in exaggerated and mock surprise, as though he were attempting to discover to whom the prefect was talking. Then he turned back to his original position. "Were you speaking to us?" he inquired.

The prefect gave him a pitying look. "No, I was talking to the bookcase behind you." Several other prefects on the same table laughed. "Of course I was talking to you. Keep quiet or get out."

Dave tried to control his rising annoyance. If he couldn't retire to the library for a spot of relaxation and trifling conversation, where else could he go, especially if they were planning to close the common room? He was aware that everyone in the library was now staring in his direction.

"If I see you talking again," continued the prefect, enjoying himself, "I shall have to throw you out of the library, and your friend as well."

"Try it," invited Dave, sitting back in his chair, "and see how far you get."

The prefect bristled with his power. It was going to be open defiance of the rules, was it? Well, he would soon see about that.

"I'm a librarian as well as a prefect," he said, pointing to a badge on his blazer lapel, "and it's my job to keep people out of here if they're going to be a nuisance. I think you'd better leave the room."

"And *I* think," said Dave, staring straight back at him, "that you can go and stuff yourself until your big fat tender backside begins to creak."

Everyone roared with laughter. This was just what they needed to brighten up an otherwise dull morning. The prefect gaped at him.

"Because," went on Dave, "I don't move myself for pompous pricks like you."

The prefect jumped to his feet.

"Are you going to force me to fetch the deputy?" he

shouted across the room.

"You can go and fetch whoever you like." Dave turned back to Brian. "Now what were we talking about when we were so rudely interrupted?"

"We were talking about ringing Miles," said Brian.

"Were we?"

"No, I was. You were out, and so was he."

"I'm really warning you," said the prefect, walking up to their table and wagging a finger at them.

"Oh, go away, you miserable specimen," said Dave dismissively in a tired voice.

The prefect turned back to his friends and fellow prefects for support, but none was forthcoming. Several of them knew Dave and they weren't going to get involved.

"I may be mistaken," said Dave, "but it appears to me that you're making much more noise than I am. I suggest that if anyone is going to leave this library, it ought to be you. Do you agree with me, Brian?"

"Yes," said Brian enthusiastically, and they both stood up quickly and caught hold of him, one on each arm. He let out a cry of protest, but there was nothing he could do about it. They marched him all around the library like some prize acquisition and threw him out into the corridor that ran along the balcony. Everyone in the room cheered, including his friends.

"I don't know about you," said Dave, turning to Brian, "but I think I've had enough of being in here."

They picked up their briefcases and removed themselves to the sixth form common room two doors along the corridor. It was full of riotous noise and cigarette smoke.

"I thought you said the common room was going to be closed," said Dave.

"No I didn't," said Brian. "I said they were thinking of closing it. Obviously it was just a rumour." He noticed a girl getting a cup of something from the coffee machine. "Look, they've even got the coffee machine working again."

Most of the activity in the room was centred around three

separate tables where various card games were in progress. The hardened gamblers sat at another table around the corner, out of sight, from where coins could be heard exchanging hands.

"If they're not going to close it after all," said Brian brightly, "I shall still be able to have my lunch in here."

"Shhhhh!" said one of the card players, glaring up at them in displeasure. "Can't you see we're in the middle of a game? How can we concentrate when you're standing there talking?"

"Sorry," said Dave hastily, knowing the true value of silence. "Come on, we can't interrupt their game."

He and Brian left the common room and began to walk slowly around the school.

"The thing that puzzles me," said Brian, "is how Miles keeps managing to borrow his old man's car."

"The way I heard it, it's quite easy," said Dave. "He brings it to school when his old man's away."

"Yes I know, but that must mean his old man's always away."

Dave shrugged. "He works for some foreign company and goes abroad a lot, from what I can gather."

"Lucky Miles."

"Anyway, what's wrong with my old woman's Mini?" demanded Dave.

"It hasn't got an MOT," said Brian, "and the way you drive around in it, it's not likely to get one, either."

"It *has* got an MOT!" said Dave in exasperation. "How many times do I have to tell you?"

"Why does your mother keep letting you borrow it if she thinks it hasn't?"

"Because I keep telling her I'm taking it to be fixed. She hasn't got a clue about these things."

"Oh." There was a short silence. "When you think about it mind, Miles didn't exactly waste his time yesterday with Francesca, did he?"

"I suppose not," agreed Dave. "She's a nice girl. Too good

for this school."

"You don't reckon...?"

"What?"

"You don't reckon he fancies her?"

"What, Miles? Fancy Francesca?"

They both looked hard at each other. Without another
word, they steered a course towards the lobby and quietly
approached the office door. It was closed. There were
sounds of movement from within, but the door had opaque
glass panels and it was impossible to make out anything other
than a vague shape inside the room. Brian took hold of the
chair that stood outside the headmaster's study, moved it
across the floor and jumped up onto it so that he could see
through the clear glass screen above the door.

"She's not there!" he whispered to Dave. "The secretary's
on her own!"

The reason that neither Miles nor Francesca was on the
school premises at that precise moment was perfectly simple:
they were both in each other's company elsewhere. In fact
they had been spending quite a lot of time in each other's
company during the past few hours, and they were both
secretly delighted that nobody else knew anything about it.
Francesca had told Miles that she was going to cycle to
school that morning, so he dragged his own bicycle out of
the shed in his back garden and rode off on it to meet her.
They met up along the way, and suddenly, by mutual
consent, their route changed and they turned off the main
road that led to the school and headed out into the
countryside. The morning was full of early sunshine and
evaporating dew.

"Help!" yelled Miles, swaying from one side to the other of
the narrow track they were following across a large
undulating meadow, "I'm falling off again!"

Francesca turned back to look at him and swung around in
a wide circle. "You're doing it on purpose!" she laughed.

"I don't know why you think this is so amusing," he said
ruefully. "I haven't ridden this thing for years. Do you realise

I'm going to fall off any minute?"

"I'm sorry, I can't help it," said Francesca. "You look so funny. It's miles too small for you."

"You mean it's too small for Miles," he corrected. The next moment he was on the grass and heading down a slope with bumps in it. "When you said let's go for a ride, I didn't think you meant this!" he shouted back to her. He pedalled back up the slope again and they carried on along the track. He glanced at her and caught an expression of blissful joy on her lovely face.

"This is very good for us, you know," said Francesca happily.

"Good for us?" repeated Miles incredulously. "I'll be lucky if I don't end up falling off and breaking my neck. How do you stop this thing?"

He tried the brakes and brought the bicycle to a juddering halt, jumping off. Francesca slowed down and stopped alongside him. She dismounted as well and they propped the bicycles against a tree. Miles leaned back against it to look around. Francesca came up beside him and he ruffled her hair. Not far away, across the fields and a busy road, they could see the school buildings. The morning traffic was making its way along the road. They were able to make out some figures on the school playing fields. Francesca found that her gaze was drawn to the office window. But at this distance, the school and all that it contained seemed very remote and unimportant.

"We're both trying to get away from it," she murmured. "That's all it is."

"Yes," said Miles, and turned to look at her. "Won't anyone miss you?"

Francesca gave a small indifferent shrug. "I don't care if they do. And no, somehow I don't think they will, not after what happened yesterday. I shall just say I was unwell and couldn't make it today."

"I suppose we're in the same position as each other, you and I," remarked Miles. "Neither of us really wants to be there although both of us know that we ought to."

She considered for a moment. "I think there is a slight difference."

"Oh yes – you happen to work there and I don't. And if the place was run properly, you would probably do the least and I would do the most."

She smiled. "Something like that."

He grinned. "Something very much like that."

"But as it is, things just remain as they are?"

"*I* can't change it."

"You could try."

He sank back against the tree, one arm around her, and gazed abstractedly into the distance. She responded by putting her own arm through his and held on to him.

"For what purpose?" he asked softly.

The silence before her response was only momentary. "That must be for you to decide." She looked at him steadily. "You know, you're a very curious boy. You have so many different attitudes."

"You said that last night."

She chuckled. "I don't mind if I say it again. Will you let me ask you one question, though? And make me a solemn promise?"

"What sort of solemn promise?"

"That you'll give me a truthful answer."

Miles hesitated. "All right. What's your question?"

"Why *are* you as you are?"

"Because it's how I *want* to be," he said after a long pause. "And nobody can ever alter me."

"They can try."

"But they won't succeed." A frown puckered his brow. "Anyway, why? Would you really like to?"

"What?"

"Alter me?"

"Yes, of course I would," said Francesca.

"But only for the better?"

"Yes."

He gave a low ineffable sigh and for once he couldn't think what to say, so he said nothing. An uneasy feeling went through him, a feeling that told him he should not be there talking like this. He felt momentarily unsure of himself again, as though he had awoken suddenly from a dream. She caught a glimpse of the serious expression on his face, the look of indeterminate puzzlement, and pulled away from him with a teasing tug on the arm.

"See if you can catch me!" she said and ran playfully around the back of the tree. He watched the movement of her lithe body, twisting itself out of his reach, and impulsively he chased after her. They went around the tree a few times, dodging to and fro, and when they got tired of that they ran across the field to the next tree until Miles managed to catch hold of her. This was not how a second year sixth-former was meant to behave with one of the office staff, but who cared?

Chapter 15

It did not take long for rumours to start going around the school. They began as whisperings among the sixth-formers, but very soon they spread to the lower forms and eventually they came to the notice of the staff.

"Have you heard what's been going on?" the question would be asked.

"No, what?" would come the answer.

"The deputy's having an affair with the secretary's secretary!"

"You don't mean it?"

A nod would follow, and so the rumour kept spreading, secretly and furtively. Brian and Dave had done their work well.

"You must be crazy," they said to Miles when they caught up with him the following day. He was walking briskly around the school, doing laps.

"I am," he said joyfully, "about her."

"It can only have one ending," warned Brian in his most doom-laden voice.

"It *will* only have one ending," said Dave with an emphatic nod of the head.

Miles stopped abruptly and looked at them. "What do you mean?" he asked.

"She's one of *them*," whispered Brian. "And before you know it, you'll be back at your lessons again – working!"

Miles was shocked.

"You're out of your minds," he protested. "What, *me?* Go to lessons? *Work?* Oh, really!" He set off again.

"Anyway," said Dave, calling loudly after him, "you have nothing more to worry about. We've taken good care of it for you."

Soon afterwards, Miles was approached by Peter, who seemed anxious to impart some news.

"Have you heard what's been going on?" he asked.

"No, what?" answered Miles.

"The deputy's having an affair with the secretary's secretary!"

"You don't mean it?"

Peter nodded. "Mind you," he added, winking knowingly, "I don't believe a word of it myself." But the rumour kept on spreading, even more secretly and furtively. In the end, Miles found himself believing it.

The deputy was used to rumours spreading secretly and furtively about him and he immediately took evasive action by disappearing into the small storeroom at the back of the library where he was reputed to keep bottles of gin hidden away for just such an emergency. There was something devilish about the deputy's evasiveness that made the rumour seem all the more secret and furtive, and before long there was no question in anyone's mind about it being anything other than the plain and simple truth. Only Francesca seemed to be unaware of what was going on, for she carried on typing in her corner of the office, completely oblivious to all the secret and furtive whisperings. Miles felt desperately sorry for her, but this only lasted until Suzanne came back into sight again, when he noticed that her hair was different and she appeared to be wearing a shorter skirt than usual. He was sitting in the library, wondering how long the deputy would remain hidden away in the storeroom, and looked up at her approvingly. She sat down beside him with a smile and he caught a delicious smell of perfume. She crossed one leg languidly over the other and swung it slowly back and fore so that the toe of her shoe touched against him. Miles sniffed the air.

"Nice perfume," he said.

"I've hardly seen you since the night of the dance," said Suzanne.

"I've been very busy," said Miles truthfully.

"Working?"

"Avoiding it."

"I don't understand you at all," said Suzanne after a short silence. "You've got exams coming soon. Why are you so lazy?"

"I'm not lazy," protested Miles.

"You are," she replied with astonishing vehemence. "You're *very* lazy."

"Well, why not? It's no great terrible sin to want to do nothing. Why doesn't everyone else behave like me?"

"Because they don't all want to do nothing."

"All right, then, why doesn't everyone else decide to do nothing? I'd have no objection."

"Because they're not all like you."

Miles felt as though they were going around in circles. "But I don't want to be like other people. Why should I? What have I done to deserve to be like everyone else?"

"Don't you like other people?" asked Suzanne.

"No."

"Why not?"

"Because they're not like me."

"But *I'm* not like you," she pointed out.

"That's true," admitted Miles reluctantly, "but I still want to do nothing." He said it with a defiant gleam in his eye.

Suzanne sighed and decided to try another day, when the same thing would happen and she would just sigh again and wait for yet another day. One day something different might happen, she kept reassuring herself, whilst Miles kept reassuring himself that nothing different was going to happen at all.

He liked Suzanne for various reasons. He even enjoyed calling her Suzanne because he liked the name, and decided that even if her name hadn't been Suzanne in the first instance he would probably have called her that anyway. He liked her perfume and he liked it when she touched him with her foot.

"I really think I'm in love with Suzanne," he confessed to Peter, who was in the art room drawing erotic pictures in charcoal.

"That's careless," said Peter, not listening very attentively.

"What is?"

"You really being in love with Suzanne. Anyway, I'll bet you're not as much in love with her as I am with this beauty here—" He jerked his thumb towards the erotic picture he was working on and smiled lovingly at it.

"Who is she?" inquired Miles, trying to look at it from all angles and wondering how Peter could possibly be so captivated by the drawing of a nude figure that defied description.

"Who *is* she?" repeated Peter. "Can't you tell?"

"No," said Miles, shaking his head sadly, "I can't tell."

"You mean you *won't* tell," whispered Peter secretively. "She doesn't know I've done it yet. It's Catherine from the fifth form. I got her to pose for a few rough sketches."

"But how did you get her to look like *that?*" asked Miles incredulously.

"Oh, I told her it was all in the interest of modern art," said Peter. "She had her clothes off before I could stop her. When she sees this," he went on dreamily, "she'll be very proud of me."

"When she sees this," said Miles, "she'll be more likely to murder you."

Peter looked taken aback.

"Do you think so?"

Miles nodded. "Wouldn't be surprised." He changed the subject. "It was a good school dance."

"Did you think it was a good school dance?" said Peter, pleased.

Miles nodded again. "It was a brilliant school dance."

"Did you think it was a brilliant school dance?" said Peter, even more pleased.

Miles suddenly felt depressed. "It was a terrible school dance," he said, changing his mind, and wandered off.

Peter went back to work on his erotic sketch until he remembered Miles's prediction and tore the picture up into hundreds of pieces, scattering them on the floor like grey confetti. "I'm crazy," he told himself, watching all the fragments fluttering to the ground.

Miles returned to his favourite place in the library where he sat thinking about Suzanne for the rest of the day. He thought about her shorter skirt, her perfume, her languidly-crossed legs and the toe of her shoe that kept touching against him. He knew she was longing to go to bed with him and he decided that he would promise to take her out somewhere one evening.

"If I promise to take you out somewhere one evening," he would say to her, "will you let me take you back home afterwards when your parents are out?"

"If I promise to let you take me back home when my parents are out, will you be good?" she would ask.

"What do you mean by that?" he demanded suspiciously in his mind, not sure whether it was going to be worth promising to take her out somewhere one evening or not. "Aren't I always good?"

"No more than I always know if my parents are going to be out," replied Suzanne obscurely.

"Why don't you ask them first and then I'll promise to take you out," suggested Miles deviously.

"Only if you promise to be good," insisted Suzanne.

"I promise to be good," said Miles, convincing himself with the truthfulness of his answer.

"Then I promise to let you take me out somewhere one evening and afterwards you can take me back home when my parents are out and then I will let you take me to bed," said Suzanne's imaginary voice in Miles's ears, and he felt a warm glow of satisfaction inside which lasted until the bell went for the end of the day. Only then did the deputy creep quietly out from the storeroom at the back of the library and return to his own room, wondering if anyone had noticed his absence. The deputy was having trouble with his wife, who was plump, middle-aged and obstinate. His wife accused him of trying to have an affair with the secretary.

"My wife must be out of her mind," he confided in the secretary one day. "She keeps thinking I'm having an affair with some fine woman in this school."

"In this school?" mused the secretary, wondering whom that might mean.

"Yes," said the deputy. "She's obviously out of her mind."

"What a pity," said the secretary. "I don't think I've ever met your wife, have I?"

"I doubt it," grumbled the deputy, thinking about his plump, middle-aged and obstinate wife. "What I could do with right now is a divorce. I feel in the mood for one. Do you think I could get a divorce if I forced myself to have an affair with some fine woman in this school?" he hinted.

"I don't know," said the secretary, wondering. "Do you think your wife would be likely to find out?"

"I suppose it could be arranged," considered the deputy, and left the matter wide open to provide new possibilities for speculation.

Chapter 16

It suited Miles to keep the school permanently puzzled because that meant they wouldn't be ready to pounce on him and ask awkward questions. In order to keep the school puzzled, all he had to do was to arrive at odd times of the day and hope that nobody saw him. It meant that he could vary the time of his arrival as much as he liked and none of the staff would be any the wiser.

He was often so late that he did not bother going into the office to pay his usual call on Francesca, who was forever having arguments with the secretary. Instead, he passed the open office door and blew her a kiss as he went by. On the days when he did not pay his usual call on Francesca, he would be marked absent on the register. This also suited him because everyone would assume that he was not in school when in fact he actually was, and this was another means of keeping them puzzled. As long as they were puzzled, he felt safe.

One day, the headmaster suddenly decided for no apparent reason that he wanted to see Miles. The headmaster didn't really want to see him at all.

"If the headmaster doesn't want to see me," said Miles, "then why does he suddenly decide for no apparent reason that he wants to see me?"

"I don't know," said Adrian, who was sitting in the library with Honey. Miles thought that she was so gorgeous he wanted to tell her he was secretly madly in love with her. He disliked Adrian because of Honey as much as he liked Honey for the way she stood on the touchline, jumping up and down excitedly in her duffle coat and boots, covering herself in mud. He immediately made up his mind that he wanted to play rugby, but Paul Brown, who was the captain of the rugby team, told him that he wasn't good enough.

"What do you mean?" demanded Miles. "I'm not good enough?"

"That's what I mean," said Paul. "You're not good enough."

"Who says I'm not good enough?" said Miles.

"Everyone who knows," said Paul.

"But I'm your friend," pleaded Miles. "Don't you remember that I'm your best friend?"

"No you're not," said Paul with a pout. "You're always telling me I need to see a psychiatrist."

"Ah yes," said Miles desperately. "But only a best friend *would* tell you that."

"Since when?" demanded Paul, and stalked off.

Miles went down to the lobby and knocked cautiously on the headmaster's door. There was a long pause from the other side before a voice reluctantly said, "Come in."

He opened the door and went into the study. The headmaster was sitting at his desk, writing busily. Miles closed the door behind him and moved quietly into the middle of the room. The headmaster continued with his preoccupied scribbling for another minute until he finished whatever it was and sat back with certain satisfaction.

He looked up at Miles and frowned.

"Yes? What is it? Do you want to see me?" he asked.

"You want to see me, sir," corrected Miles.

"How do you know I want to see you?" countered the headmaster. "Did anyone tell you I wanted to see you?"

"Yes, sir," said Miles, "someone told me you wanted to see me."

The headmaster looked glum.

"I suppose I'd better see you, then."

"Thank you, sir. I thought you probably would."

"Did you?" said the headmaster, even more glumly. "What's your name?"

"Miles Randolph, sir."

"Randolph? Do I know you?"

"I don't think you do, sir," said Miles, and added helpfully, "I don't play rugby, sir."

"Oh no, I remember now, you're the one I don't know because you don't play rugby."

"That's right, sir. I'm the one you don't know because I don't play rugby. I imagine that if I did play rugby, you would know me very well, and I was only thinking to myself earlier that perhaps I ought to start playing."

"What do you want?" asked the headmaster obtusely.

"You wanted to see me, sir," repeated Miles heavily, thinking that the conversation was going to last for a very long time.

The headmaster sighed in resignation. "Randolph, my boy, I never want to see *anyone*. I'm told by the deputy that I want to see someone because he never wants to see them himself. It's his job to see them because I'm much too busy to see them myself."

"Yes, sir, I can see that, sir."

"But he never agrees with me."

"What did you want to see me about, sir?" asked Miles patiently.

"I didn't want to see you about anything," said the headmaster in surprise.

"What did the deputy want you to see me about, sir?" asked Miles, trying a different approach.

"I didn't even know the deputy wanted me to see you until he came and told me," grumbled the headmaster. He picked up a handwritten sheet of paper that was lying on the desk in front of him and studied it for a while. Occasionally he would shake his head slowly and make tutting noises. Sometimes he might even purse his lips tightly together and open his eyes wide. Finally he put it down again and muttered, "Dreadful. Shocking. Quite appalling. A report here of yesterday's match. I don't know what we're coming to. Now then, where was I? Oh yes, we were talking about you, weren't we? Well, tell me, have you been working hard?"

"Yes, sir," lied Miles without a particle of shame, "very hard, sir."

"Unfortunately it appears that some of the staff think otherwise." The headmaster consulted another report which had been given to him earlier by the deputy who was standing in the office, pretending to examine the registers. Francesca thought that he was spying on her and went off to complain to the secretary, who was waiting impatiently to tell the headmaster that Francesca had been rude to her again.

Miles felt desperately sorry for Francesca. He was sure she was being persecuted by the secretary, who wanted to get rid of her. The headmaster couldn't care less about Francesca because he was feeling desperately sorry for himself. He was sure that he was being persecuted by the deputy, who wanted to get rid of him. The headmaster was a very suspicious man.

"This report isn't good," he said, looking up at Miles. "Physics: 'Hardly ever attends, but whenever he does, he spends most of his time sitting at the front of the laboratory talking.' Chemistry: 'Rarely comes to class, but on the days I see him he seems to sit at the back of the laboratory talking.' I mean, what is all this talking about?"

"Oh, work, sir," said Miles reassuringly.

"Hmm. Pure mathematics: 'Haven't seen him all term.' Applied mathematics: 'Who is Miles Randolph?'"

"It's me, sir," said Miles. "I find maths very difficult."

"You might find it easier if you went to your lessons more often."

"I did actually want to take biology, sir," said Miles helpfully. "That probably has something to do with it."

"Biology? Biology?" said the headmaster. "Whatever has that got to do with it?"

"I wanted to be a doctor, sir."

The headmaster scrutinised the report. "It doesn't say

anything here about you taking biology."

"It wouldn't, sir," said Miles. "I don't."

"Then why mention it?"

"Because it's the subject I wanted to take but the school wouldn't let me."

"I fail to understand why that should have anything to do with the progress report on the subjects you *are* taking," said the headmaster.

"It has a lot to do with it, sir," said Miles. "I didn't want to take maths, I wanted to take biology. The school told me I couldn't take biology because there wasn't any room in the class so it made me take maths instead."

"That hardly explains your poor attendance in physics and chemistry," said the headmaster sternly, looking at Miles over the top of his spectacles.

"Doesn't it, sir?" said Miles.

"It's time we saw you making more effort."

"Yes, sir."

"Do I make myself understood?"

"Of course, sir."

"There's no excuse for not working just because you can't take all the subjects you wanted to."

"Biology was a rather important one, sir."

"They're *all* important."

"I suppose they are, sir," said Miles, feeling depressed.

"There's no suppose about it," said the headmaster dismissively, and waved the matter to a conclusion with his hand. "That's all."

"Thank you, sir."

"I don't know why the deputy couldn't think of that himself, without having to get me involved." The headmaster felt suitably sanctified after seeing Miles. Miles felt disagreeably sick after seeing the headmaster. It meant they were watching him after all. He left the study and went outside to see if Honey was anywhere about. Instead, he found Suzanne waiting for him.

"What happened?" she asked breathlessly.

"The headmaster wanted to see me," said Miles in surprise. "Why?"

"What did he want?"

"He wanted to tell me something," said Miles.

"What did he want to tell you?"

"He wanted to tell me I've been expelled," lied Miles happily.

Suzanne stared at him in disbelief.

"Miles!"

"It's true."

"It can't be!"

"Absolutely. No doubt about it. Chucked out, and that's it."

"But—"

"It's come as a dreadful shock, mind, but I suppose I'll soon get over it."

"But why?" she asked imploringly.

"Why? Oh, um, well they found out I was the one who wrote that limerick on the poster for the school dance."

"They didn't!"

Miles nodded. Suzanne shook her head miserably.

"Is that it now?" she wanted to know.

"Is that what now?" asked Miles, equally as intrigued.

"Does this mean it's the end...for us?" She had a sad expression on her face and he felt sorry for her without any idea why she felt sorry for him.

"Do you want it to be?"

"No, of course not!"

"Well then." The bell rang loudly throughout the school for the change of lesson and pupils began making their way through the lobby on their way to different classes.

"I've got a lesson now," she said.

"Bad luck," he said sympathetically.

"I've really got a lesson," she insisted.

"That's really bad luck," he insisted with more sympathy.

"Miles, I might never see you again," said Suzanne dramatically.

"That's true," said Miles. "You might never see me again. I might never see you again either."

Suzanne began to cry.

"Please don't cry," he said, trying to soothe her.

"Why not?" she replied, sobbing over him. "Can't I cry if I want to?"

"I suppose so, if you're sure you want to," said Miles. "But I hate to see a grown girl crying."

"Why should you hate to see a grown girl crying?" she wept, peering blearily up at him. "Is there any reason why a grown girl shouldn't cry if she wants to?"

Miles knew he would never forgive himself for making things up like that and upsetting her. Perhaps if he could never forgive himself she would forgive him instead.

Before Suzanne found out that he hadn't really been expelled at all, several days passed during which time Miles decided to make the most of his new-found freedom. He thought that he would prowl around all of his favourite haunts before making up his mind where to settle. He noticed Lisa sitting in a corner of the sixth form common room, all alone. She was a big girl and she had dark hair and golden-tanned skin. Her eyes were big and dark, too, and she had long eyelashes. Lisa spent a lot of her time sitting in her corner by the window, looking out, with a faraway expression on her beautiful face. Miles wondered vaguely if she never worked, like him. She always had a book open on her lap, but that didn't mean anything. It just meant she could read, and it didn't necessarily mean that either, although he suspected that she probably could.

"Do you ever read that book?" he asked her one day, after waiting for ten minutes to see if she turned over a page.

"Of course I do!" she snapped, and turned over a page.

He watched her cross her legs and pull her short skirt up an inch or two.

"Is there any point just sitting there pretending to read that book?" he asked her judicially after waiting another few minutes to see if she carried on reading.

"What are you trying to imply by that question?" she asked coldly.

"No more than I implied with the other question," answered Miles innocently, and gazed up and down the length of her legs. She wore a pair of black high-heeled court shoes, and he decided that she had very nice ankles. He fell in love with her immediately and smiled at her every time she glanced up in his direction to see if he was still going to smile at her every time she glanced in his direction.

"Don't you ever do anything except sit and do nothing?" she inquired after a while. He moved closer to her to see if she would draw away from him or stay in the same position. She remained where she was.

"I devote my time to accomplishing a higher ideal than work," he explained loftily.

She regarded him dubiously. He reached out and stroked one of her breasts and she shrieked.

"I'm not sure I understand," she exclaimed, recovering her composure. Miles stared at her in wonder, from the pointed toes of her shoes to the long dark hair that fell down over her shoulders, and felt sorry for anyone who couldn't get close enough to touch her. At first she was reluctant to do anything other than watch him cautiously. By the end of the week, she was lively and eager.

"Why don't we go somewhere quiet?" suggested Lisa when she decided that the common room was much too noisy for her liking.

"Where shall we go?" asked Miles. "It's quiet in the library."

"There are too many people in the library," said Lisa.

"Where else can we go, then?" said Miles. "It's quiet in the physics darkroom."

"I don't take physics," she said.

"I can't think of anywhere else."

"We could go somewhere quiet like my home," she said temptingly.

"I don't know where your home is," said Miles.

"All right, then," she snapped. "Don't take me home this afternoon and I won't let you undress me in my bedroom in front of a big mirror."

"If I take you home this afternoon and you let me undress you in your bedroom in front of a big mirror, what do we do afterwards?"

"You can admire my naked body," she said.

"What do we do after that?" asked Miles.

"After that you can make love to me," she said.

Miles began to like the sound of Lisa's suggestion. "I've got a good idea," he said. "Let me take you home this afternoon so you can let me undress you in your bedroom in front of a big mirror and then we can make love."

She pursed her lips and thought about it for a moment.

"No," she said at last, and Miles ran out of the common room to go and duck his head under the shower.

Chapter 17

Instead of going to duck his head under the shower, Miles went to see Miss Williams the young teacher who had taught him O-level French in the days when he used to work very hard before he decided he wanted to learn biology. In the first year sixth he kept going to her class secretly during the games lessons to study biology on his own whilst she was giving extra tuition to Arnold who wanted to be a linguist. Miles even had his name on her class register, although he would have preferred to be in the proper biology class, which the school wouldn't let him join. Miss Williams was pleased to have his name on her register, even if he never turned up for French lessons with the intention of doing anything except read about biology, and now he was only too pleased to be doing neither one thing nor the other.

Miles never discovered Miss Williams's first name because he was too polite to ask, so he just called her Miss instead, because she didn't have a ring on her finger until the day he bought her one as a present for being kind enough to have him in her class and not try to teach him anything. He liked Miss Williams so much that he deliberately failed his French O-level so that he could take it again. The school suggested that he should forget about French and concentrate on his sixth form subjects. When he asked if he could take biology in the sixth form as they had promised he could because he wanted to be a doctor, they said no, the class was too big already. So Miles decided to forget about the whole lot.

But he didn't forget about Miss Williams. He decided that she liked him to visit her in the French room because he was the only person in the school she understood properly; he was so open and honest in his constant effort to avoid work that she probably wondered if he was the only sane person in the entire world. He used to go along to her room and surprise her when she wasn't in the middle of giving a lesson to anyone. Arnold used to be jealous because they talked and laughed together at her desk by the blackboard whilst he was sitting at the back of the room learning vocabulary and he taunted Miles by reminding him that he had passed his French O-level examination and Miles had failed it.

"So who's laughing?" demanded Miles.

"I am," said Arnold, pretending not to.

"I never wanted to pass it anyway," said Miles haughtily.

"Oh no?" said Arnold, sniggering. "Why did you take it in the first place, then, if you never wanted to pass?"

"So that I could throw myself at Miss Williams every time she felt like enjoying my company while you slaved over your books and tried to ignore us," answered Miles truthfully.

"Oh yes?" replied Arnold, still sniggering. "Stupid."

Ever since that time, Arnold considered Miles to be a complete imbecile who not only didn't know his own mind but also didn't know anyone else's, either. But Arnold no longer went to see Miss Williams, he had gone past that now. Miles had Miss Williams all to himself whenever he called to see her these days and she was the only person in the school who could advise him without making him think of Minus Davies.

"Do you know," he said to her one day, "you're the only person in the school who can advise me without making me think of Mr Davies."

"Who's Mr Davies?" asked Miss Williams, not sure whether she had ever heard of him before.

"Who's Mr Davies?" repeated Miles in surprise.

She nodded.

"Yes, who is he?"

"He's just a careers master who tries to teach some kind of rudimentary mathematics to the remedials who don't want to learn it anyway, or can't," explained Miles. "In his spare time he advises us about careers. He hides himself away in his little room on the balcony."

"I don't even know him," confessed Miss Williams. "Is it really possible for me to be unaware of his existence in this school when he's a member of the staff like me?"

"It seems as though it is," surmised Miles. "But perhaps he's as much unaware of your existence as you are unaware of his. In which case I assume that you cancel each other out."

"What a dreadful thought," she whispered in horror. "I don't like the idea of being cancelled out. It has such an air of finality about it."

"Do you believe in justice?" he asked.

"Yes," she said. "Why do you ask?"

"I just wondered if there was any such thing. If there wasn't, I suppose you wouldn't believe in it."

"I *like* to believe in it," she said, correcting herself.

"There must be an awful lot of people in this world who don't believe in it," said Miles with a deep sigh. "Do you know why I wanted to take French?"

"Yes, because you wanted to take something else instead but they wouldn't let you so you came to my class to study it in secret."

"They?" queried Miles, opening his eyes wide.

Miss Williams coughed and tried to avert her gaze.

"We."

"You."

"Not me. Others. Them."

"Them is us," said Miles. "Them is *you.*"

Miles liked Miss Williams because he could have arguments with her and she never minded. She was a young woman, still in the full bloom of early adulthood, and she had a pretty face and light brown hair. She wore sensible rather than fashionable clothes, usually a plain skirt and jumper and shoes with flat heels. He guessed that she probably had some exciting parts to her but they were kept well out of sight, which was a shame. The day he went to see her instead of going to duck his head under the shower, she was preparing some work for the first year sixth and after spending only a few minutes talking to her, he headed back up to the library, pleased that he had successfully avoided going to physics.

On the way there, he bumped into Mr Collins the academic registrar who had long ago given up teaching Miles geography and who was now looking for him to find out why he never went to any of his lessons. Mr Collins was a large man with a broad, expansive personality and he carried himself with a precise, upright, military bearing. In his younger days he might well have been a regimental sergeant major.

"Don't you know there's a process of education going on all around you while you just sit back and do nothing?" boomed Mr Collins in a voice that was capable of reaching every corner of the school.

"Yes, sir," said Miles, wishing that he would talk more quietly.

"Don't you have any idea why taxpayers' money goes into building schools like this?" roared Mr Collins, who was very keen.

"Yes, sir," said Miles meekly.

"Don't you ever stop to think of what you're doing to *yourself?*" raged Mr Collins, resplendent in his black gown and mortar-board.

"Yes, sir," said Miles timidly.

"What conclusions do you come to about it?" shouted Mr Collins in despair.

"I'm quite happy to know that taxpayers' money goes into building schools like this, inside which there's a process of education going on all around me while I just sit back and do nothing," recited Miles.

"Oh, that's *very* good!" congratulated Mr Collins sarcastically.

"Thank you, sir."

"And don't say thank you sir like that."

"No, sir."

"That's better."

"Thank you, sir."

"I said don't say thank you, sir."

"No, sir."

"That's much better," said Mr Collins. "What subjects are you taking?"

"I'm not taking biology, sir," said Miles.

"Why not?"

"I wasn't allowed to, sir. The headmaster said the class was already full enough and there wasn't any room for me."

"We can't always take the subjects we want to, you know. It's just not possible."

"Can't we, sir? I thought the school was meant to let the pupil decide on what subjects to take."

"In any case," said Mr Collins, "there's always an alternative."

"Is there really, sir?"

"Of course there is! What are you taking instead of biology?"

"Pure and applied maths, sir. It's not quite the same as biology, sir. They don't give you a place in medical college without biology, sir."

"Who wants a place in medical college?" asked Mr Collins in complete bafflement.

"I did, sir."

The academic registrar went on his way without the remotest idea of what Miles was talking about. Miles continued on his way to the library, where he settled down at his usual table. John was sitting nearby.

"Have you done all your physics homework?" he asked Miles.

"What physics homework?" countered Miles with raised eyebrows.

"The stuff we were given last week."

Miles gave a disinterested shrug. "I hardly ever go to physics."

"That's not a very good excuse," said John.

"If you hardly ever went to physics either, you'd think it was an excellent excuse," said Miles evenly.

And so it was. If he went to physics, he was given homework. If he was given homework, that must have meant he had been to physics. If he wanted to avoid going to physics, all he had to do was forget about his homework and if he had not been to physics in the first place, he would not have been given homework anyway. It was as simple as that.

"It looks as though you might be in trouble," said John persistently. "Mr Bates never knows where you are. One day he's going to order you to go to physics."

The next day, Miles went to physics as ordered and nobody noticed he was there. Mr Bates never saw him whether he was there or not and it made Miles cross. He had been tricked. He rounded on Mad Mike, who had only called on Miles to ask him a favour.

"I don't want to do you any favours," snapped Miles irritably.

"Will you let me borrow your log tables in the exam?" asked Mad Mike. "I've lost mine."

"What exam?" asked Miles.

"The exam for which I want to borrow your log tables," said Mad Mike.

"Why do you want log tables?" asked Miles. "Can't you use your brain, like everyone else?"

"It's not awfully useful without log tables," said Mad Mike apologetically.

"Do you think you can go through life with a book of log tables and they'll solve all your problems for you?" sneered Miles. "Is that it?"

"I only want them for the exam," promised Mad Mike. "You can have them back straightaway afterwards."

"What happens if I want to use them myself?" demanded Miles.

"Then you could borrow somebody else's," said Mad Mike brightly.

"Oh, what a brilliant idea! Tell me, how do you propose to let my log tables solve all your problems for you?"

"By helping me to pass the exam," said Mad Mike. "Then I might get to university."

"That's when your problems *begin*," replied Miles. "If you want my advice, forget it."

Mad Mike began to look alarmed.

"I don't want your advice," he stammered. "I just want to go to university and be a success in life."

Miles shuddered.

"In that case I would forget about logarithms if I were you. They won't help one little bit."

"Why do you have to say things like that?" quailed Mad Mike querulously. "You make me feel so insecure and a failure before I've even tried."

"That's better than feeling a failure *after* you've tried," said Miles. "Believe me, I know."

"I don't think you know anything," complained Mad Mike bitterly.

"That's how I'm going to fail," beamed Miles. "You see? It *does* work!"

Mad Mike went off to duck his head under the shower instead.

Chapter 18

Peter knew as much about art as Miles knew about dodging work, which all depended on how much work Miles was able to dodge without being detected. Peter was tall, thin and forever energetic, and he had the uncanny ability to persuade girls to fall over themselves backwards to do whatever he wanted them to in his wild, frantic, unceasing search for perfect art. He got them to parade their lovely naked bodies in front of him while he pretended to sketch them or draw them or paint them and always managed to ask them out afterwards, when they had put their clothes back on again.

Peter lived alone in the art room and not many people knew that he existed. The deputy suspected because he had suspicions about most things, but he was never able to prove absolutely in his mind that Peter really was part of the school and therefore subject to the rules and regulations governing pupils' behaviour, which did not include drawing erotic pictures of nude girls.

Peter fell easily into moods. Bad moods came easiest of all, and he got into bad moods when he was bored. He got bored with sitting in the art room every day drinking mugs of foaming white coffee which one of the plump fifth form girls used to make for him in the hope that he would start fancying her. Hazel was a nice enough girl and Peter liked her very much but because he only liked her instead of fancying her, he got bored with that too.

Victoria was Peter's permanent model and he fancied her

very much because she did everything he ever asked her to do. She was a tall slender blonde girl, willowy and delectable, yielding and acquiescent to his every whim and command. She had short hair and wore large gold ear-rings to taunt some of the mistresses into demanding that she took them off. She had become Peter's model by wearing clothes that were not part of the school uniform and took them off too. Peter went with her to a nightclub in Kingshampton every Friday evening and didn't know that Miles had a secret yearning for her as well. One Friday night, Miles arranged to be at the same place at the same time after making sure that Peter had mysteriously been sent elsewhere.

"I'm a friend of Peter's," said Miles, introducing himself to her by the side of the dance-floor where she was standing alone, looking around for Peter. "Are you a friend of his, too?"

"Yes," she said.

"He said he couldn't come tonight," said Miles, shouting to make himself heard above the raucous sound of the music. "He asked me to come instead." He smiled at her and she smiled back. "What's your name?"

"Victoria," she answered.

"I'm Miles."

She laughed.

"That's a funny name."

"It's not as funny as Arnold," said Miles.

"Do you know Arnold?" she asked in surprise.

"No, who's Arnold?"

"You don't know him?"

"I might know him if it paid me to," said Miles, thinking of Arnold's sister who had a friend with nice big tits, "but he only wants to be a linguist and I think that's boring."

"What do you want to be?" inquired Victoria.

"I want to be a success," said Miles dazzlingly. "I propose to achieve success by not being a failure."

Victoria looked at him with an expression of uncertainty.

"How are you going to do that?" she asked.

"By not failing when the time comes, by not doing any work, by not knowing whether I would have failed if I *had* worked when everyone told me to," said Miles.

"How fascinating," said Victoria, stifling a bored yawn. "Why couldn't Peter come tonight? He always takes me out on a Friday night."

"He said he had to go somewhere else," said Miles.

"He didn't tell me."

"Bad luck," said Miles. "Would you like a dance?"

"All right," agreed Victoria, and they made their way out onto the dance-floor where they had a dance. It was fast and exciting and Miles enjoyed the aimless fury of it.

"Would you like me to take you home afterwards?" he asked when it had finished and they were both gasping for breath and covered in perspiration.

"I don't know yet whether I like you or not," said Victoria, pushing her hair back.

"Pretend I'm Peter," suggested Miles.

She laughed. "All right, Peter, you can take me home afterwards. Can you draw?"

"Of course," said Miles. "Who can't?"

"Peter can't," said Victoria. "He thinks he can, but everyone knows he can't."

"Don't you ever tell him he can't draw?"

"Oh no! He wouldn't believe me anyway. Can *you* draw better than him?"

"I don't know how well Peter can't draw," said Miles. "But I suppose I'm pretty good."

"What are you like with girls?"

"Ask them."

"I'm asking myself."

Victoria made up her mind that she liked Miles and decided to introduce him to her friends. Whenever she saw someone she knew, she brought them over and introduced Miles as Peter, and just to confuse matters more she told them that Peter was Miles.

"This is Peter," she kept saying, and Miles smiled sweetly

149

and whispered quietly to them behind her back, "It's Miles actually." He enjoyed watching their puzzled stares and curious sidelong glances.

"This is Peter," said Victoria to one girl who told Miles that she was Victoria's best friend.

"It's Miles actually," corrected Miles. "And you can't be Victoria's best friend because Peter is."

"You're Peter?" asked the girl.

"No, I'm Miles. Peter's Peter but he's not here tonight."

"You're spoiling it," said Victoria crossly after her best friend had gone off again.

"Why should I be Peter?" demanded Miles. "I don't want to be him! Let him be himself, and if he can't draw properly that's *his* fault, not mine."

"But you suggested being him in the first place."

"Only so that I could take you home afterwards, and to prove that I *can* draw."

"Which he can't?"

"Exactly!"

"Will you draw *me* one day?" asked Victoria pleadingly. "I'm so fed up with being drawn by Peter all the time."

"If you like," agreed Miles. "When?"

"When you take me home," she said with a satisfied smile.

One day, the deputy got all the evidence he needed. He found Peter sketching an erotic picture and hauled him off to see the headmaster.

"Did you do this?" demanded the headmaster, looking at it with his eyes wide open, hardly able to believe what he was staring at.

"No sir," said Peter, "I didn't do it."

"If you didn't do it, then who did?" asked the deputy aggressively.

"I know who did it," said Peter brightly. "It was Miles."

"Don't know him," said the headmaster shortly, sitting back in his chair.

They confiscated the erotic picture and let Peter go back to the art room. Hazel, the plump girl from the fifth form who had become Peter's helper, hopeful that some of his artistic talent might rub off on her like charcoal or chalk-dust, made him another mug of foaming white coffee to cheer him up but after he had drunk it he didn't feel in the mood to do any more drawing so he left the art room to go up to the library where he saw Miles being led away by two prefects who told him that the deputy wanted to see him.

The deputy wanted to see him so that he could get all the evidence he needed to have Miles thrown out of the school because he secretly suspected that Miles was up to something. He took Miles into his room at the side of the lobby and asked him if he could draw.

"Can I draw?" repeated Miles abstractedly.

"Yes, can you draw?" demanded the deputy.

"What, sir?"

"Anything that's relevant to the reason I want to know," said the deputy evasively.

"What is the reason you want to know, sir?" asked Miles cautiously.

"Never mind why I want to know, that's irrelevant!" said the deputy irritably. "Just answer what's relevant and don't answer what's irrelevant."

"How will I know if it's relevant or irrelevant, sir?" inquired Miles politely.

"I'll tell you," the deputy assured him.

Miles nodded.

The deputy opened the drawer of his desk and peeped at the erotic picture which he had taken from the headmaster's desk at lunchtime. He coughed and quickly closed the drawer again in case Miles wondered what he was looking at.

"What can you draw?" he asked.

"I can't draw anything, sir," confessed Miles.

The deputy boggled at him. "Who said you can't draw anything?" he roared.

"I did, sir," said Miles meekly.

"That's irrelevant! Of course you can draw! I know you can! I've even seen what you've done!" The deputy calmed down and took another look in the drawer. "You can admit anything you like to me, that's what I'm here for."

"Can I really, sir?" said Miles gleefully.

The deputy nodded.

"Yes. Anything you like."

"That's very kind of you, sir."

"I'm a very kind man."

"But I haven't got anything to admit," admitted Miles.

"Why not?" shouted the deputy angrily.

Miles made a hopeless gesture. "Because I haven't done anything to admit to, sir."

"You're in trouble," warned the deputy. "I can tell you now, you're in serious trouble. What's your name?"

"Peter, sir," said Miles. "I'm Peter."

"They told me you were Miles Randolph," grumbled the deputy.

"Who's he, sir?" asked Miles blankly.

"Never mind. I don't want to see you if your name's Peter and not Miles Randolph. Where can I find Miles Randolph?"

"I should imagine you might well find him in the art room, sir," said Miles. "He spends most of his time drawing erotic pictures of naked girls in the fifth and sixth forms, so I expect you will find him down in the art room doing just that."

The deputy sprang out of his chair to go and find Miles, who was Peter, down in the art room. When he arrived, he only found Peter, who was not Miles, drinking another mug of foaming white coffee and he felt so utterly confused by it all that he retreated to the library and hid himself away in his little storeroom until the end of the day. Miles spent the rest of the afternoon in the office with Francesca, helping her to sharpen pencils using a pencil-sharpening device that was fixed to one end of the desk and operated by turning a little handle. He sharpened them all down to nothing and soon the waste-paper bin was full of wood shavings.

"Miles!" exclaimed Francesca when she saw the growing pile. "Whatever are you doing?"

"I *was* thinking of changing my name," said Miles, "but I don't think I'll bother any longer. I think I'll just get rid of all the pencils in the school instead and then nobody can do any more drawing."

Chapter 19

In Miles's opinion, the girls in the sixth form could be divided into two categories. There were the pretty ones who knew how to make the best of themselves, who had the right poise, the good looks, the whole essence of attractiveness, and there were the others, the plain and awkward ones who seemed to have no idea, no graceful way of presenting themselves, who walked about in groups of unprepossessing ugliness, as if they had no interest in the matter. Miles shrugged to himself. Perhaps they didn't care, and if that was the case, why should he worry about it? After all, there were some girls he liked to look at and there were others he couldn't stand the sight of. It went both ways and he could think of quite a few boys, thin and fat, pimply-faced, chinless or oafish, who must have made many a girl despair. That was life, and as far as he was concerned there were some girls who set his pulses racing and there were others who practically froze his blood.

Julie, Helen and Dawn came into this second category. They always went around together and Miles felt rather sorry for them. They were known affectionately as the Three Ugly Monsters. It had nothing to do with their size or their build or the length of their hair or the shape of their legs, it was no one thing in particular but there was something in the way they had been created that put him off. He was sure they had many fine qualities if one looked hard enough, but he was not particularly interested in looking. They probably had all the requisite bits and pieces in the right places and there must be some poor boy in the school who would find them quite beautiful.

Brian?

Miles was worried about Brian's lack of success with girls and decided that he needed some help and immediately he thought about the Three Ugly Monsters. What better way could there be to initiate Brian into the delights of sexual gratification than to fix him up with one of those? The question was, how? Miles began to have an idea. He started by dropping hints.

"Look at the Ugly Monsters, Brian," he would say whenever he, Brian and Dave were sauntering aimlessly around the school at breaktime. The three girls often stood by the noticeboard outside the lobby, reading the school notices, or at least making a reasonable pretence that they were studying them. Actually they stood there so that they could watch all the boys going past. Miles's circuit of the school deliberately included walking through the lobby.

"I don't want to look at them," said Brian in horror after they had gone past and heard the three girls giggling.

"They're fine young women," said Miles. "Aren't they, Dave?"

"They certainly are," agreed Dave, nodding his head enthusiastically.

"Untouched, I should say," said Miles.

"Untouchable," said Dave in agreement. "Anyway, they're *girls*, aren't they? You keep saying you want a girl."

"Not one of *those!*" said Brian, aghast.

"You could do a lot worse," said Miles encouragingly. "Tell you what, I've got an idea." He whipped a set of poker dice out of his pocket. "We'll play for them. The loser has to ask one of them to go out with him for the night. That's fair, isn't it, because we each have a chance of losing. Come on."

Miles and Dave steered Brian firmly into the assembly hall and headed for a vacant window-sill. During the daytime the hall was occupied by lower years who were placed in there whenever a teacher was absent. It was a repository for untaught classes. The only unoccupied window happened to be the one nearest to the doors leading out into the lobby. Poker dice were regarded by the school as being more corrupt and degenerate than a pack of playing cards and it amused Miles to think that they would be rolling their five dice within earshot of the headmaster's study.

Of course, Brian didn't stand a chance from the beginning, for Miles and Dave had planned this between them and although they could not be certain of beating him every time, the eventual outcome was assured. Royal flushes and full houses swept past his bemused gaze but Brian's throwing of the dice could not match theirs and by the end of breaktime he was beaten. Miles peeped out through the window and saw that the three girls were still in their usual place in the corner of one quadrangle.

"They haven't moved an inch from where they were standing," he said and gave Brian a nudge. "Which one do you fancy the most?"

"Dawn's a big girl," said Dave. "Just look at the size of her tits. You could get lost in those."

"Julie's a large lass, too," pointed out Miles. "A bit too heavy for me. But I'm sure she's a very nice girl when you get to know her."

"And what about Helen?" said Dave. "Not the most beautiful girl in the world, maybe, but she's got that look in her eyes. You can tell she's ready for it."

"Ready for what?" asked Brian in confusion, looking from one to the other. "Now come on, boys, you don't *seriously* expect me to go up to them and ask one of them to go out with me, do you?"

Miles looked at him sternly.

"You agreed to abide by the conditions of the game and you've lost. Off you go."

"B-b-but—" stammered Brian.

"It's no use protesting," said Dave. "It could have happened to any one of us. Personally I rather like the look of Helen, she's got a cute little nose."

"But I can't just walk up to them like that!" said Brian, appalled. "What do I say?"

"Oh, you're hopeless," said Miles impatiently. "Come here and tell me, which one of them do you like the look of the most?"

Brian stared miserably at them through the window for a long time.

"Dawn," he said at last with a heavy sigh.

"Wait here," said Miles and left the hall. A few moments later Brian could see him stepping out into the quadrangle and approaching the three girls. He began talking to them and they gathered around him to listen. Brian couldn't hear what he was saying, but the girls started exchanging glances with each other and the look of surprise on their faces soon changed to nods and giggling smiles. Miles then reached forward, took Dawn by the hand and led her into the hall. Brian felt the colour draining from his face and the four walls seemed to start closing in on him and spinning around. He was aware that his eyes were staring wildly and his head had begun to throb horribly. He felt as if he were shrinking inside himself, overcome by some dreadful numbness. And all the while, words seemed to be coming out of Miles's mouth and he had to force himself to listen.

"Dawn, this is Brian," said Miles by way of introduction. "He was too shy to ask you himself, but he says he would like to go out with you. Brian, this is Dawn."

Dawn, who stood in height not far short of Brian, looked at him with a big smile on her face and her eyes were shining. He stepped back against the wall but it prevented him from retreating any further. Suddenly she came up to him, put her arms around his neck and gave him an enormous kiss.

"I'll go out with you any time you like," she said, looking at him in admiration. "I thought you'd never ask!"

"I didn't," he said weakly.

"I've fancied you for ages," she went on breathlessly.

Brian recovered slightly.

"Er, have you?"

Dawn nodded. He looked at her more closely. She had come alive in front of him and he saw not an Ugly Monster but a young girl with passion and fire in her blood. Pretty? Well, not quite, but not that bad, either. In fact, the more he studied her, the prettier she became. He drew himself up to his full height and started to feel rather pleased with himself. He had a girl at last. She might not be a raving beauty, but there was *something* in her looks that pleased him. And she had actually *kissed* him. There was hope for him yet.

"Where shall we go?" he asked.

"Wherever you like," said Dawn. "I can be ready soon after teatime."

"Where shall we meet?"

"Wherever you like," she said. "I can be outside my house at half-past six."

Miles stepped back and drew Dave to one side.

"Did you see how much she's changed?" he whispered. "She's a different girl all of a sudden."

Dave nodded.

"I could almost fancy her myself," he said, looking her up and down. "Well, maybe not."

The bell rang for the end of breaktime and Miles slipped the poker dice back into his pocket. He and Dave made their way up to the library where they spent the rest of the morning while Brian walked around in a blissful daze.

Chapter 20

Brian's parents were not very well off financially. His father worked as an accounts clerk in the office of a builders' merchant and his mother had a part-time cleaning job. The family owned one car which was an ageing black Hillman Minx. It was almost as old as Brian and he could not hope to compare it with Miles's father's company Rover or Dave's mother's Mini, so most of the time he kept quiet about it. In his opinion it was something of an acute embarrassment and he preferred to walk to school, even in the pouring rain, rather than be seen sitting inside such an antiquated old wreck. His father was very proud of it and got it out of the garage each weekend to clean and polish it. The family couldn't afford proper driving lessons with an instructor for Brian when he reached the age of seventeen, so his father put L-plates on the car and taught Brian himself. He must have done a reasonably good job of it too, because Brian passed his driving test first time, but pride prevented him from borrowing the car very often, he was so ashamed of it.

He did not let on to his friends in school about it. As far as they were concerned, he did not drive. He even preferred them to believe that his family did not own a car at all. On the other hand, Dawn was a girl and girls did not generally show much interest in cars so long as they had *something* to travel about in.

At exactly half-past six, Brian carefully steered the Hillman Minx into Dawn's street and pulled up outside her house. His father's exhortations were still ringing in his ears: "Bring it back in one piece and remember to behave yourself!" Brian had washed his hair, brushed his teeth and put on his best casual clothes. Dawn waved to him from her lounge window and presently came out through the front door. Brian watched her walk down the garden path towards him and blinked. Was this the girl he had shied away from in school? He looked at her again. Gone was the school uniform and in its place she wore a short plaid skirt and a loose-fitting woollen cowl-necked sweater, dark tights and a pair of smart high-heeled shoes. Her hair was tied back in a pony-tail and she had applied make-up to her face. She had a small fawn-coloured leather handbag slung over one shoulder which matched her shoes. She seemed to sense Brian's reaction and smiled at him when she got into the car.

"Is this better?" she inquired, gesturing to her appearance.

"You've taken my breath away," said Brian in admiration.

"I wanted to look my best for you," she said coyly.

Brian tentatively engaged the gears and they set off down the road. The springs of the car creaked under their combined weight, for there was no doubting that Dawn was a hefty lass, and Brian, although rather slim, was very tall. Between them, they seemed to fill the front seats of the car and it looked as though it had been designed for somewhat smaller occupants.

"Where do you want to go?" he asked.

"I don't mind," said Dawn. "You can decide."

"I thought we could go to the cinema."

"Let's do that," she agreed.

There were three cinemas in the town centre and they went to the one showing a *Carry On* film and squeezed themselves into two seats in the back row. Once the lights went down and the short began, they had their arms around each other and Dawn started smothering Brian with kisses. In the darkness she had her leg across his lap and he had his hand across the back of her thigh. The film went unnoticed; only the sound of laughter from the rest of the audience reminded them that it was still running and when they got to the interval, Brian's head was spinning. "What a girl!" he kept thinking to himself. By the time the *Carry On* film got under way Dawn had taken off her bra and Brian nuzzled rapturously into her ample breasts. They could hardly wait for the film to end before racing back to the car. It was dark and rain was falling.

"Let's find somewhere quiet," said Dawn, her passion aroused, and Brian drove out of the car park at a speed that the Hillman Minx had never once experienced in all its years of sedate motoring. Its narrow cross-ply tyres struggled to get a grip on the wet road and they skidded and slid their way to a lane that ran near the town's municipal playing fields. Trees and rough ground loomed in front of the car's headlights and Brian brought it to a halt in a small clearing. Rain dripped off the tall overhanging trees and pattered on the roof. What happened inside the car can only be imagined, for in its cramped interior there was very little room for a rather large girl and a tall, long-legged boy to manoeuvre themselves. Their efforts were not helped, either, by the simple fact that the seats would not recline but remained obstinately upright. In the end they scrambled into the back, their clothes flung everywhere, and Brian discovered that when Dawn brought her entire weight bearing down on top of him he was hardly able to breathe. The poor car must have wondered what on earth was happening to it and after half an hour both it, and they, were thoroughly exhausted. While Brian and Dawn lay dozing contentedly in each other's arms, headlights shone in the lane behind them and a car approached slowly and drew up alongside. If the windows of the Hillman had not been so steamed up, Brian might have recognised the familiar outline of a white Rover 3500 saloon car, but as far as he was concerned he was floating in dreamland with the most lovely girl he could ever wish to meet. He had fallen hopelessly in love.

A loud knocking on the car window jolted him awake and he leapt up suddenly. Dawn moaned quietly beside him and pulled him back towards her.

"Stop it!" he whispered frantically. "There's somebody outside!"

"What?" she squeaked and grabbed her clothes.

"Open up in the name of the law!" called out a deep gruff voice.

"It's the police!" squealed Dawn, trembling. "What are we going to do?"

"Keep your head down out of sight and they won't see you," said Brian and reached across to wind the window down. He lowered it two or three inches and peered out into the darkness.

"Hello," greeted Miles cheerfully. "Having fun?"

"Miles!" said Brian hoarsely. "You bastard! What are you doing here?"

"I was out for the evening with Suzanne," said Miles. "We were at the cinema too, but you left so quickly we lost you." Brian could see Suzanne sitting in the front passenger seat of the Rover, illuminated by the glow from the instrument panel. She waved to him.

"Have you been following us?" asked Brian incredulously.

"Yes, to begin with," said Miles. "But you proved to be too fast for us. I say, this is some car you've got here, wherever did it come from? Anyway, we've been searching everywhere for you, and then Suzanne, the clever thing, suggested trying here. And here you are! Well, sorry to disturb you and all that – I reckon we'd better be getting along. Apparently Suzanne's parents are out tonight so we thought we'd go back to her place. Good night."

Brian closed the window and felt the radiant warmth of Dawn against him. She pressed her lips to his and pulled him back down. "Wait until they've gone," she whispered in his ear, "and then we'll do it again."

"It's about time Brian got himself fixed up with a nice girl," said Miles, starting up the Rover's engine.

"They seem to be having a good time," said Suzanne, running her finger down Miles's leg.

"I'm surprised he knows what to do," he confessed.

"Perhaps she's showing him."

"I'm surprised *either* of them knows what to do."

"Don't underestimate her just because you used to make fun of her and her friends. She's got that look in her eye. You can tell."

"What sort of look?"

"This one." She stopped moving her finger and said in a husky voice, "Let's go."

Miles engaged the gears and swung the car around. In the dim light of the interior, he glanced at Suzanne. All evening he had only seen her as a shadowy silhouette, either in the cinema, sitting beside him at the far end of the back row from where Brian and Dawn were seated, or inside the comfortable cockpit of the Rover. He had not so much seen her as scented her, the freshly-washed hair, the musky perfume that she had applied to herself afterwards, the odour of femininity. He reached out for her hand and gave it a gentle squeeze.

"Isn't it wonderful to be free?" he said. "We're like two free spirits, you and me. Two free spirits who have the whole world to ourselves. No school because it doesn't exist, it's not there any more. We've banished it from our lives for ever."

"Until tomorrow morning," Suzanne reminded him with a sigh. She watched the beam of the headlights shining on the road ahead and the hedgerows on either side and, beyond that, the blackness of the night. Perhaps there really was nothing else out there, perhaps they really were all alone in their own little private existence. She took his hand and let it touch her. She had her legs tucked up beneath her and he firstly felt the leather of her boots and then the soft smooth surface of her thighs and she kept guiding his hand upwards between the folds of her dress. "But we've got all of tonight to ourselves."

"So we have," said Miles and his voice was quiet and thoughtful. "Let's not talk about tomorrow."

163

They drove to Suzanne's house in a quiet leafy avenue. When they arrived, the house was in darkness and silence. The road, too, was dark and silent, with small pools of light formed every so often by the glow from old-fashioned street lights, the sort that used to be lit by a gas-mantle before they were eventually converted to electricity, and Miles pulled up at the kerb. The rain was still falling in a fine misty drizzle. They got out of the car and ran, hand in hand, up the drive to the front door. Suzanne fumbled in her handbag for her key and the next thing Miles knew, they were standing inside the large hallway.

"We're in!" she said breathlessly. "Come on!"

"Wait a minute," said Miles cautiously, holding her by the arm, "when are you expecting your parents back?"

"They said they were going to be out late," said Suzanne, "and my brother's away at university, so we won't be disturbed. Now come on, follow me. I'm not going to put the lights on, so be careful you don't fall over anything." He felt her fine warm young body pressed against him for a moment and then she turned and pulled him forward after her. He followed her across the hall and she led him up the wide staircase to the landing, lit only by a thin pale light that came in through the windows from the street lamp outside the house. They crossed the landing and she took him into her bedroom and closed the door. She put her arms around his neck and began kissing him and Miles responded by kissing her back more fervently. She sank onto the bed and he settled down beside her and their kissing reached an ever greater intensity.

"Undress me," she instructed him in a whisper and lay back. In the darkness, Miles could hardly see. He felt her with his hands. She had her legs apart and he unzipped her boots and took them off, dropping them on the soft carpet. Then he unfastened her dress and slipped it off over her shoulders while she unbuttoned his shirt and undid his trousers. He reached for her bra but she said "you'll never undo that" and undid it for him. When they were completely undressed, he stared at her in the grey dimness of her room and said, "Suzie, I think you're absolutely beautiful."

She put a finger to his lips.

"No more talking," she said quietly. "I want you to be very *very* good."

It was some time later when a car pulled up outside the house. Its engine made a loud noise and the headlights cast a patch of brightness onto the bedroom ceiling above the curtains. Miles sprang up.

"What's that?" he gasped in panic.

"A car," murmured Suzanne drowsily, lying beside him with a feeling of deep satisfaction.

"I know it's a car!" he said. "But what's it doing outside? Are you expecting anyone? Could it be your parents back already?"

Suzanne propped herself up on one elbow.

"It's not the sound our car makes," she said. "Daddy's got a Granada and it makes a low *rrrrrrm*. And if it's anyone else, I shan't let them in so you needn't worry."

"I should think not!" said Miles. "You've got nothing on!"

"Does it matter?"

"What? That you've got nothing on?"

"No, silly, I meant does it matter who's outside? They'll probably go away again in a minute. Cuddle me, I'm getting cold." She reached out her hand and pulled Miles back to her. A few seconds later they could hear the car driving away. "There you are," she said sleepily, "what did I tell you? It's gone."

Miles began kissing her again and stroking her until she breathed deeply with pleasure.

"Up a bit," she said. "Mmmmm, that's nice." And then, after a while, she spoke again in a thoughtful voice. "Miles…"

"Yes?"

"What do you want out of this world?"

He paused to consider the question.

"How can I possibly know what I want when I don't know

any more where I'm going?"

"That's not a proper answer."

"It's the only answer I can give."

"But you must want something. The way you're going at the moment, you'll end up with nothing. You must surely want something out of life."

"Apart from you?" Miles shrugged his shoulders in the dark. "I did want something once, I wanted it very badly. It was a thing I had set my mind on for years."

She ran her fingers idly over his chest. "What was it?"

"Nothing that matters any more. They wouldn't let me take a subject at A-level that I needed to take, so I never had a chance. What else was there for me to do? How could I replace one ambition with another while the first remained but was no longer possible? I couldn't."

"I'm sorry, I never realised."

"I didn't imagine you would. There aren't many people who *do* know – or care."

"What about your two friends?"

"You mean Brian and Dave? Yes, they know, but they're idle layabouts anyway. Perhaps we *all* are, deep down and at heart, but some of us are better at getting away with it than others."

They both fell silent. Then Miles laughed, and for a long time he lay there next to her, laughing.

"What's the matter?" asked Suzanne anxiously.

"Oh dear," he said, "it's not really funny at all. It's just us, like this. We were in the school library this afternoon and you were sitting there so prim and proper with your books spread out on the table in front of you, working hard and looking very scholarly. What does it all mean?"

"It means—" she began to say, but suddenly they heard the sound of a car again, stopping outside. Its engine kept running and it gave a loud toot on its horn. "Oh God, it *must* be my parents! They've left the car there and had a lift back! What shall we do?"

Miles leapt out of bed and went to the window. An old car

stood on the road outside, partly hidden by the garden hedge, but enough of it showed for Miles to see Brian sitting in the driver's seat, waving up at him. Dawn sat beside him, looking up as well. Brian wound the window down and shouted, "Did we interrupt something? Terribly sorry!"

Before Miles could open his mouth to reply, Brian crashed the gears together and sped off.

"It's that bastard Brian and his Minx!" he raged.

Chapter 21

"How did you get on last night?" asked Miles the following morning.

"I thought she was going to kill me," said Brian. Miles had the feeling that he looked somewhat flatter than usual about the chest and stomach, as though he had been squashed and not yet popped back to his normal shape. "She wouldn't get off me and I was gasping for air. I thought I was a goner. What a girl!"

"What a way to go," whistled Miles with a wink of one eye. "So you had a good time on your first night out together? That's marvellous."

"How about you?" asked Brian after a pause. "Did you get on all right?"

"Yes, when she let me," said Miles.

They looked at each other and both grinned at the unspoken thought of a shared experience. It was the first lesson period of the day and the library was quiet.

"I don't know about you," said Brian ruefully in a low voice, "but I'm feeling a bit sore today."

Miles chuckled.

"You'll get used to it," he said. "The main thing is, do you feel any different?"

"I feel very tired. My mother could hardly wake me this morning. Then I nearly fell asleep again over my corn flakes. I'm sure she suspects something, and I could hardly look my father in the face. Mind you, he was only concerned about the car."

"He should have given you a long talk on the subject," said Miles wisely.

"Oh, he did once," said Brian. "I know exactly how the engine works, and the steering and brakes—"

"Not the car, you idiot! On the subject of girls!"

"He's never mentioned *that*."

"Neither has mine, come to think of it. I doubt if most fathers do. And then you wonder why you've become one yourself." Miles sighed. "*C'est la vie*."

Brian began to look alarmed. "You don't think so, do you?"

Miles raised his eyebrows in despair. "Well, that depends if you did anything more than kiss, doesn't it!"

Brian dived into his briefcase and pulled his chemistry file out and started reading it. Miles peered over and noticed that he was holding the file the right way around and every so often he turned a page. This was beginning to look serious. He heard Brian muttering words like "benzene ring" and "atomic number", and he glanced at the scribblings on the paper. It seemed as though Brian was trying to make up for lost time.

Dave came into the library after a while but Brian did not appear to notice his arrival: he was deep in a chemistry trance. Dave sat down opposite Miles.

"What's got into him all of a sudden?" he asked, nodding towards Brian.

"I'm not sure if it's infatuation or exhaustion," said Miles sadly, "but whatever it is, this friendship with Dawn seems to have gone to his head. It's making him work."

Dave pulled a face.

"That's bad," he said. "Now if there's one thing that my friendship with Jane has never done, it's to make me work. I don't see why it should. We have a very good arrangement: she works hard all day in her little shop in town and I laze about in school. What more could a young chap want out of life, apart from a few beers now and then?"

"Brian's only just discovered he's in love," said Miles. "Give him a bit of time and he'll probably soon be back to his usual idle self."

While Miles was worrying about Brian, Brian was worrying about Dawn who kept reminding him about the examinations a long time before they were due to begin and how he was crazy not to realise how important they were.

"What if I fail?" stammered Brian nervously.

"You're not going to fail," Dawn assured him kindly in a voice that had steely determination laced with silkiness, and Brian turned pale at the thought of impending doom.

"Tell me what happens if I fail," he begged her. "Will I be lost for good?"

"Tell me what happens if you *pass*," grumbled Dave, who cured the problem by devoting more and more of his time to sleeping at his favourite table in the library, during which time he was able to relieve his mind of all the pressures and doubts that examinations so cruelly bred and nurtured. He didn't have Jane to keep worrying him all the time because she was safely ensconced in her small boutique and only spoke to him in the daytime when he rang her from the school office while Francesca was busy talking to Miles. Dave avoided the subject of examinations in the same way that he would have avoided Miles if Miles had been the sort of person who went around preaching the virtues of idleness and then working secretly behind everyone's back. But Dave knew that Miles wasn't like that and could be relied upon to fail well when the time came.

Suzanne decided that the time had come to take Miles firmly in hand.

"How long do you think you can keep going on like this?" she asked him in despair one day.

"As long as I like," replied Miles, not caring.

"Miles, don't you even *care* about it?" she asked him incredulously.

"No," said Miles, "I don't even care about it."

"But you must do! Would you care about it if I promised to

go to bed with you again?"

Miles gave the matter some thought.

"That's not fair," he said. "You know very well I'd say yes to that because anything's worth caring about for you."

She blushed.

"Do you mean that?"

"You know damn well I do."

"What possible reason do you have for wanting to fail?" asked Francesca suddenly when Miles joined her in the empty canteen later that day when she went to get herself a cup of tea instead of typing a letter from the headmaster to herself which the secretary had dictated to make it look as though it had come from the headmaster when in fact Francesca knew perfectly well that it hadn't come from the headmaster at all because she had gone into the study to ask him and he had said no in order to avoid becoming involved in yet another argument.

"Because I don't want to pass," said Miles.

"What possible reason could you have for not wanting to pass?" asked Francesca, deeply worried by his attitude, stirring her cup of tea. "It just doesn't make any sense."

"It makes plenty of sense to me," said Miles. "I'm afraid of exams."

"But Miles, why should you be afraid of exams?" asked Francesca, so concerned by his attitude that she stopped stirring her cup of tea and began drinking it.

"They hurt," said Miles. "Haven't you noticed how much they hurt? Ever since I started taking them, they've always hurt me."

"How do they hurt you?"

"Hasn't it occurred to you that all examiners do is try to destroy people's simple belief in themselves that they are better than the next person? How else can you have that simple belief shattered and destroyed more effectively than by failing an examination in a subject in which you have been striving for so long to prove yourself?"

"But if you *pass* the exam, it doesn't shatter your faith in yourself. It gives you more confidence."

"*If*," muttered Miles. "That's a big word, isn't it, for just two letters. Anyway, there's more to it than that."

Francesca shook her head. "Look, Miles, you're wrong."

"No, *you're* wrong."

"We can't both be wrong."

"We could be," considered Miles.

"You just want to keep arguing about everything all the time—"

"Francesca," said Miles impulsively, interrupting her, "I love you. I do, really, ever so much."

"No you don't, Miles," she said hastily, lowering her voice and looking around quickly to see if there was anybody nearby. "You might think you do but you don't, any more than I love you. Oh, I *like* you, certainly I do, but that's not the same thing, is it?"

Miles gazed into her dark eyes with great sincerity.

"I wish you were younger than you are," he confided.

"I wish a lot of things myself," sighed Francesca, "and that's one of them. But it doesn't alter the situation."

"Do you wish you were younger than me?"

She laughed.

"Of course I do! Wouldn't you, if you were me?"

Miles kissed her on the cheek and ran off happily, knowing that Francesca could always be relied upon to cheer him up in his moments of pessimism, despondency and gloom. At lunchtime he went up to the common room where Dave was sitting cosily with Lisa who was temptingly demonstrating to him how she had wickedly teased the deputy by pulling up her skirt, and Dave threw his arms around her with abandon and told her how he thought she was so gorgeously arrogant and totally unprincipled. He loved every moment of her tempestuously extravagant company and she loved every moment of his because he promised to take her out when Jane wasn't around.

Lisa pouted when she saw Miles, and Miles didn't make a grab at one of her delightful breasts in case it made Dave cross. Instead, he sat down beside them and started to get worried about Brian again.

"I'm worried about Brian," he told Dave confidentially.

"Why?" asked Dave in surprise. "What is there to be worried about?"

"I'm worried because he's afraid," said Miles.

"What's he got to be afraid of, apart from Dawn squashing him?"

"He's afraid he's going to fail his exams. She keeps reminding him about them, even though it's ages before they begin. She still keeps reminding him and I don't think he knows what to do with her."

"It's a shame," said Dave sympathetically. "Poor Brian."

"Who's Brian?" inquired Lisa.

"Just a friend," said Dave, "who's afraid he's going to fail his exams. I don't know what he's got to be afraid of. Didn't you know we're all going to fail our exams?"

Lisa began to look intrigued.

"No," she said. "Are you really?"

"Yes, we are really," said Dave. "Aren't we, Miles?"

"No doubt about it," grinned Miles.

Lisa regarded him with cool disapprobation. "It's hardly worth your while coming to school then, is it?"

"Of course it is!" replied Miles indignantly. "We've got lots of other interests. Haven't we, Dave?"

Dave nodded.

"Yes, lots," he said in agreement.

And yet Miles could not entirely rid himself of a small feeling that had crept into his mind and begun to grow. It was a feeling of unease. It had not been caused by anything that had been said to him by the headmaster or the deputy or any of the teachers. In fact, it was almost indefinable and possibly something that he had imagined. But it was there all the same, a tiny nagging doubt, and he did not like it.

One day he walked around the school on his own for a while and took a small hard-backed notebook from his blazer pocket and turned over the pages slowly where he had methodically written line after line of chemical equations and reactions, physics definitions and all kinds of mathematical formulae. He read through them, remembering the time he had taken to copy them all out when no one was looking; he recalled the thoughts within himself when he was doing it and pondering on the thing that had motivated him more than anything else.

There *was* no justice in the world, he decided. Not when his academic life could be sacrificed for so little.

On his travels around the school he lost all count of time when, without warning, a window slid open above him and two heads appeared.

"What are you doing down there?" asked Brian, leaning out of the library window.

Miles came to a halt and gazed up.

"Whatever it is," he said cryptically, "it's the opposite to what you're doing up there."

"We're very busy," said Dave with a grin.

Miles laughed softly. "Yes, of course." He consulted his notebook and then called up to them, "What's the first law of thermodynamics?"

"That's the one that comes before the second law," said Brian intelligently.

"Do you know?"

"Of course not!" said Dave irritably. "What are you reading that rubbish for?"

Miles wondered. Why *was* he reading it? He felt as though he had just awoken from a very confusing dream. But it was a dream that he had shared something very special with Suzanne, a wonderful, exhilarating dream of togetherness and since it had happened, nothing had been quite the same.

Chapter 22

Miles was sitting in the library, pondering. Cogitating. He was trying to explore his innermost thoughts. If he could tell what he was thinking then he could probably discover a means of working out what was happening to him. So he spent a long time with his eyes tightly shut, meditating. The sun shone in through the windows, bathing him in its warm glow. Whilst he had been independent and self-assured, he knew he did not have to work because he would get on without it. He could do anything he wanted, achieve any success, pick up any girl he desired. But now he had Suzanne, and doubts were beginning to creep ever more into his mind.

What made it so different was that they had become lovers. She was no longer merely another girl in the sixth form whom he had fancied on a passing whim, admired for her tits and her legs. Suzanne had become a part of him and he had become a part of her, they had shared a part of themselves with each other and she now carried a part of him within herself, although there was no means of knowing the outcome. But it had *changed* things.

It was during this prolonged period of intensive mind-searching that Brian came into the library and sat down nearby. He watched Miles for several minutes before Miles realised that he was there. Eventually Miles sensed his presence and opened one eye.

"What are you doing here?" he asked. "Where's Dawn?"

"She's gone to a lesson," said Brian in a quiet voice. "What are you doing?"

"I was working," mumbled Miles. There were books on the table in front of him.

"What is it?" Brian glanced across at the books. "Oh, physics."

Miles suddenly banged one of the books shut and sat back. "Did you know," he said, "that the Simple Pendulum has a period of oscillation of two pi square root l over g? This is only a very close approximation, though."

"Is it really?"

"Yes. And before you came in, I was looking at the spiral spring."

"Were you?" said Brian.

Miles nodded. "But of course the spiral spring has a different period of oscillation from the Simple Pendulum because you've got to take account of the mass, small m, which hangs from the end of it. Depressing, isn't it?"

"What is?"

"That we're supposed to fill our heads with all this knowledge when you'd rather be with Dawn and I'd rather be with Suzanne."

Brian looked around.

"Where's Dave?"

"Probably with Jane or Lisa. Or maybe he's gone somewhere for a beer."

Brian gestured towards the books.

"Does this mean you've given up?"

"I don't know."

"Before I had Dawn and you had Suzanne, everything seemed different, didn't it?" said Brian. "I mean, we didn't care."

"I still don't," said Miles defiantly. "There are bigger considerations than simply fucking your girlfriend."

Brian looked taken aback.

"Are there?" he asked.

"To me there are. I gave up for a reason, not because I wanted to. I gave up because the bastards forced me to, because they took away everything I ever wanted to be. And to what end? What good has it done me, or you for that matter, or Dave?" Miles pushed his books away from him in disgust. "I ask you, what *are* we doing here, trying to cram all this useless information into ourselves? That's the question I've been asking myself all year, and there's no answer to it. So I've taken the easy way out. But then Suzanne comes along and I can't get her out of my mind. She's there all the time, possessing me, consuming me and because I love her, I *want* to be possessed and consumed and a whole lot more. Do you understand?"

Brian nodded.

"I feel the same way about Dawn. I think she's gorgeous, but it doesn't end there. She's started telling me what to do." Brian lowered his voice. "She thinks you're a bad influence on me."

"She may well be right," sighed Miles sadly. "I probably have been a bad influence. But let me tell you something else. If ever anyone asks me to account for myself, I intend to say *exactly* what I think of the whole bloody lot of them, and to hell with the consequences. In the meantime, I intend to keep everyone guessing, including you!"

The best thing about the staff was the way they were always holding staff meetings during the day because these gave Miles the chance to go home early without being noticed. The deputy was the only member of staff who made a special effort to catch Miles going home early without being noticed because the deputy had a strong theory that Miles was secretly planning something and he wanted to make sure that he didn't miss finding out what it was, but whenever Miles slipped out of school early he always managed to go without the deputy noticing. Miles, of course, wasn't actually planning anything except a more efficient way of ensuring that he didn't do any work, and even that strategy was beginning to waver.

"But Miles," said Miss Williams the nice French mistress who had once tried not to teach Miles French so that he could study biology on his own instead, which the school refused to let him take, "suppose nobody worked?"

"But they *do*," said Miles, "and if they didn't, I'd be pretty stupid to be any different, wouldn't I?"

"That's beside the point."

"What *is* the point?"

"Haven't you ever thought what would happen if you *did* work?"

"*If* I work hard and pass an exam, I don't prove that I'm any better than anyone else who works just as hard and passes the exam better than I do," explained Miles. "If I work hard and don't pass an exam, I prove that I'm better than anyone else who works just as hard and fails the exam worse than I do. If I *don't* work hard and fail an exam, I reckon I've proved that I'm just as good as anyone else who works hard and passes the exam and therefore the less I work, the more I prove it."

"Exams serve to compare people's ability when they pass," said Miss Williams.

"So why can't they serve to compare people's ability when they fail?" demanded Miles reasonably. "It's far easier to fail than to pass. What's wrong with making things easier instead of harder?"

"Because you're not meant to do that," said Miss Williams patiently.

"And why aren't you meant to do that?" argued Miles.

"Because you alter the standard that way."

"What standard?"

"The standard that's set to compare people's ability."

"And who sets the standard?" asked Miles.

"The examiners who decide on those who should pass and those who should fail."

But Miles wasn't in the mood to be impressed.

"So my fail could just as easily be a pass when they decide some day to alter the standard."

Miles didn't really mind most of the staff because they had no reason to bother him and he could exchange idle frivolous

178

talk with any of them provided they didn't ask awkward questions or try to inquire how he was getting on. If they did ask awkward questions or try to inquire how he was getting on, he usually adopted a different personality in order to convince them that they had got hold of somebody else by mistake because they rarely remembered him from one day to the next.

There were some members of staff whom Miles hardly knew at all, like Mr Shaw the English master who tried to coax as many first year sixth pupils as possible into taking a Use of English examination, which Miles thought sounded a bit of fun. Mr Shaw was young, unmarried and wore metal-framed spectacles which he took off when he wasn't teaching. He was also kind and generous. In his spare time he played tennis on the town's tennis courts in the park, and he was so kind and generous that he gave a lift home in his old Ford Cortina every afternoon to Nicola, who was in the fifth form and was Mr Shaw's favourite pupil. Sometimes he was so kind and generous that he used to give her extra tuition in the evenings, all for nothing, and her parents got worried about it and went to the school to see the headmaster. The headmaster didn't know anything about it until the deputy told him that her parents were coming to see him, whereupon he clasped his hands over his eyes and moaned like a man in torment. He locked himself in his study and ordered the deputy to deal with them.

One day, Miles hit upon a brilliant new idea. Instead of missing every lesson he could by spending the time in the library or going home early, he decided to attend every lesson with all the appropriate books and files and pretend to act normally so that nobody would know any different. With his new scheme in operation, Miles simply couldn't fail not to do any work. Everyone looked at him with a revised respect and Miles merely shrugged it off by picking up a book and reading it. Nuclear fission, Statics and Dynamics, he appeared to devour the lot. He devoted himself to applied mathematics at least twice a week and pure mathematics just as often.

Mr Craig the pure mathematics master was so pleased with Miles's encouraging performance that he wrote reports on him which he sent to the headmaster who was too afraid to read them but sent them on to the deputy instead who handed them over to the secretary, and all the secretary had to do was give them to Francesca who put them in a box-file with all the other reports. Francesca was the only person who read them, apart from Mr Craig and all the other teachers who wrote reports about Miles at various intervals when it suited them.

Every now and then, they tested Miles by asking him questions which Miles knew that he couldn't answer. These tests proved to be a major obstacle and he found that the most convenient way of showing how much he knew was to pretend to show how much he didn't know, which was easy, and make them think that he was being patently modest. Miles discovered that he could keep fooling the staff into eternity. Some days he seemed to be working, other days he swotted in the library. Nobody could ever prove that he didn't do anything, not even Minus Davies the careers master who sat in his tiny room near the sixth form common room and felt disillusioned at the way bright young people kept passing him by.

Easily the worst thing about pure maths was Smith, and easily the worst thing about Smith was the way he persistently dogged Mr Craig with smart answers to questions before the questions had even been asked and everyone was meant to think he must be very clever. Philip Rosser whistled aimlessly to himself and gave off an unpleasant smell which Miles put down to the fact that he probably didn't wash properly, whilst Barbara sat in front of Miles and exuded a delightful whiff of perfume which nearly drove Miles out of his mind every time she turned around to borrow his small ruler which he always kept in his blazer pocket to lend her every time she asked for it. Brian sometimes went to pure maths and hated every minute of it.

"I hate pure maths," he kept whispering to Miles.

"Who doesn't?" replied Miles, looking in his briefcase for a pure maths textbook which everyone else was using to work out problems.

"What are you looking for?" asked Brian.

"A textbook, so I can work out these problems."

"You must be mad."

"Who isn't?"

"I'm not," declared Brian proudly.

"What are you doing in pure maths, then?" challenged Miles.

"I'm not doing anything," said Brian.

"Then why bother to come?" demanded Miles.

"So that I can watch everyone working hard in a subject which I hate and realise how lucky I am not to be doing it."

"But you *are* doing it."

"Prove that I am," said Brian.

"Prove that you're not," said Miles.

"I'm under no obligation to prove anything," said Brian haughtily.

And neither was Dave under any obligation to prove to them when they wouldn't believe him that he drank beer in his local pub every evening, any more than they believed that he spent the night with Jane, his girlfriend. Actually, Dave didn't go to the pub every evening to drink beer instead of getting on with his homework which nobody bothered to set him, because he had Jane to care about. Jane worked in her small boutique in town and Dave adored her completely, so much that he was afraid to admit it, even to himself. Sometimes he slipped quietly out of school by himself to go and visit her in the little shop, which was situated in one of the quaint old timber-framed buildings at the top end of the high street. It was full of expensive and fashionable ladies' outfits, and the inside of the shop was very dimly lit by four small spotlights shining down from the low ceiling onto the clothes racks. Jane was tall, slim and sophisticated, and kept her long dark hair tied back so that he could take her quietly into one of the tiny changing rooms at the back when the manageress wasn't looking, and kiss her passionately behind one ear and down her neck, and she would respond in delight by humming sensuously and taking her clothes off right down to her lacy black panties that he had bought her as a present.

"One day I'm going to let you marry me," she told him in a whisper, "but not yet."

"What if I'm too young?" asked Dave hesitantly.

"So? One day you'll be too old. Who decides?"

"But what if I don't want to marry you when the time comes?"

"You will," Jane assured him with determined confidence. She was twenty-one and when he asked her when her birthday was she wouldn't tell him but kept it to herself, delighting in its secrecy; so she always remained twenty-one and Dave never asked her any more how old she was. Instead, he took her out in his mother's old Mini which his mother didn't use because Dave always told her it hadn't passed its MOT, which was actually as true as the fact that it hadn't failed its MOT either but his mother was too nervous to drive it again and meanwhile Dave knew it was as safe as could be. It was so safe that he never bothered to fix the faulty brakes and sometimes he gave Brian a lift to school in it which Brian always accepted gratefully because Dave's driving terrified him so much and Brian loved to feel terrified of Dave's driving.

"Do you like my driving?" demanded Dave, taking a corner much too fast.

"I think you're the worst driver I've ever been with," answered Brian, and Dave was pleased.

"Jane likes my driving too," he said proudly. "She tells me I should never have passed my test because I drive like a lunatic and I tell her that's all right because I haven't."

Brian blinked.

"Are you telling me you haven't passed your driving test?"

"Of course not!" said Dave scornfully, turning to look at him. "What's the point of taking my test if I know I'm going

182

to fail it?"

"But—" began Brian in astonishment.

"I ask you, what's the *point* in taking it?" demanded Dave. "Most people can drive well enough to pass their driving test, but there aren't many who can drive as badly as me, so I might as well not bother taking it in the first place. Jane says that in her opinion I shouldn't really be on the road, but I haven't crashed yet, have I? Anyway, my aunt never even had to take a test in her day and she's no worse off for it, so why should I be?"

Brian swallowed hard.

"So you haven't got a driving licence and the car hasn't got an MOT?" he said.

"If you look at the windscreen," said Dave, "you'll see that it hasn't got any tax, either. Jane thinks it's all great fun, but she's that sort of girl. You should see us when we're driving back from the pub after a night out! It's wild!"

"But what happens if you're stopped for drinking and driving?" asked Brian in dumbfounded amazement.

Dave gave him a withering look.

"What *can* happen?" he inquired nonchalantly. "I haven't got a licence to lose, have I? Anyway," he added, "the brakes don't work properly, so they'd have a hard job stopping me in the first place." The little Mini careered up the school drive and nearly mowed down the gardener, who jumped out of the way and shook his fist at them. Dave hooted with laughter. "I say, did you see old Harry leap into the bushes back there? I nearly had him! You won't tell anyone, though, will you?"

"Tell anyone what?" gasped Brian, looking back at the school gardener hopping up and down.

"About me and Jane. We're always having arguments because she wants to marry me, but I can't get married yet, I'm too young."

Dave rarely had arguments with Jane at all, any more than she wanted to marry him. He just wanted people to *believe* that she did, in the same way that he wanted Brian to believe that he hadn't passed his driving test. It suited Dave's perverted sense of humour, his taste for the outrageous and the bizarre.

Chapter 23

One morning Miles arranged to call for Suzanne at her house and take her to school in the car. He arrived at twenty to nine but there was no sign of her waiting outside. He got out of the car and went to ring the front door-bell. A few moments later, Suzanne rushed to open it, holding a cereal bowl in one hand and a spoon in the other.

"I overslept," she said breathlessly. "I'm sorry."

"You'll be late for school," said Miles, looking at his watch; he knew that she liked to be punctual.

"I've nearly finished," she said, stuffing more cereal into her mouth and munching it. "Come in while I go and get myself ready."

Miles stepped into the hall and she dashed off barefoot to the kitchen and put the empty bowl down on the worktop with a loud clatter. Then she ran upstairs to brush her teeth in the bathroom and fetch her schoolbag from her bedroom. She ran down the stairs again, stopping to put on her black high-heeled leather boots by the front door.

"Ready!" she gasped and called out, "Bye, mum!"

"You don't have to rush around on my account," said Miles with a grin, "I'm nearly always late anyway."

They drove to school and Miles parked the car in its usual place. They were certainly late. At least, Suzanne was; Miles, by his reckoning, was quite early. The headmaster drove past them in his car, making him even later than they were, except that didn't matter. He stopped the car, wound down the window and looked at Miles.

"School starts at ten to nine," he said sternly, consulting his watch, "and it's now nine o' clock."

"I'm sorry, sir," said Suzanne apologetically, "it's my fault. I got up late."

The headmaster ignored her explanation and kept his eyes fixed on Miles.

"You seem to think you can come and go whenever you like," he said.

"But sir," protested Suzanne, "it's got nothing to do with Miles."

"Of course it has!" said the headmaster, raising his voice. "He's brought you to school late. Make sure it doesn't happen again." He went on his way.

"I don't believe it!" she exclaimed.

"I do," said Miles in resignation. "He doesn't like me because I cause trouble. I'm a troublemaker. Now do you understand?"

"But I told him it was my fault and he completely ignored me!" said Suzanne.

"The man is an incompetent old fool," said Miles. "I know it and now you know it. But until today you didn't know, because he hides himself away in his study and you hardly ever see him. How do I know?" Miles took hold of her hand. "Follow me."

He led her around the school, which was quiet because everyone was in assembly.

"Where are we going?" she inquired.

"I want to show you something," said Miles. They walked around the quadrangle, through the lobby and headed for a corridor which took them towards the new building, a later addition to the original part of the school which was occupied by various classrooms on three different floors. On the top floor was the biology room. They climbed the stairs and went through the double doors that brought them to it.

Miles opened the biology room door. There was nobody inside.

"Go in," he invited, standing back to let Suzanne walk in first. He followed her into the room and closed the door behind him. "Welcome to the biology room. Have a good look around, there's plenty to see."

The room was already familiar to Suzanne because she had taken biology once herself before realising in form three that she wanted to give it up. A skeleton still stood by the blackboard and there were several anatomical diagrams pinned to the walls showing the internal organs, muscles and nervous system of the human body. A human skull with a detachable cranium rested on top of one shelf and on the next shelf down there was a large jar containing a preserved brain standing beside a giant plastic half-section of an eye mounted on a stand. Many more exhibits were placed inside glass cabinets that ran along the length of the room. Chalked on the blackboard, in exquisite detail, was the respiratory system of a rabbit.

"Why have you brought me up here?" she asked.

"Because I wanted you to see the room that I'm not allowed to enter," said Miles. "If you go around counting them, you will see that there are thirty-two stools, which is about the size of the O-level class. When we had to choose our subjects for O-level at the end of the third form, I put down biology because I had decided that I wanted to study medicine. But on the day of the end-of-term exam, I was ill so I missed it. For that reason, the biology master decided that I should not go into his class in spite of the fact that I desperately needed the subject. He said the class was already full and there was no room for me. My father rang the school to speak to the headmaster about it, but the old bastard was never available so in the end my father made an appointment to come in and see him. Instead of backing me up, the headmaster just said that it was the biology master's decision and he couldn't overrule him. So I missed the chance to take my O-level in the subject and that meant that I couldn't go on to take my A-level in it either. Then I had an idea. Why not take the O-level exam on my own? Surely I could study biology outside school, without the need to attend the class that they wouldn't allow me in? My father came back to ask them and they reluctantly agreed that it was possible. But they wouldn't let me do it in form four or form five. Wait until the first year sixth and do it then, they said, and perhaps we'll let you into the A-level class on the strength of it. That seemed quite reasonable, so my parents arranged for me to have private tuition and I would sit the exam at the end of that year. However, when I went into the first year sixth, they changed their minds. You can't take your A-level in biology if you haven't already passed your O-level, they said, so you'll have to take mathematics instead, but never mind, you might still get a place in medical college. I went ahead with it anyway and studied privately for my O-level – my parents arranged for me to have a two-hour session every Saturday morning at the home of a biology teacher from another school, and I used to sneak into Miss Williams's French class during the games lessons and sit at the back, reading all my biology books – and I even took human biology as well and passed them both. But it was too late by then."

Suzanne stared at him and at last she said, "I had no idea that was the reason."

"What would *you* have done in my position?"

"I don't know," she replied in a small voice.

"Would you have carried on, disregarding the fact that all your hopes and ambitions had just been crushed and destroyed by the very people who are supposed to care about you? *Would* you?"

"I don't know! I don't know!" Suzanne began pacing up and down the room. "It just doesn't seem worth destroying the rest of your life because of it. You're not affecting anyone but yourself, and you're denying yourself the chance of an alternative. You can't go on forever, doing nothing."

"Why not?" demanded Miles.

"Because you'll never keep a girl for long if you carry on as you are!" Suzanne stopped in front of him and gazed into his eyes. "Oh Miles, don't you see what you're doing to yourself?

And to those who love you?"

He took a deep breath.

"You're making it very difficult for me," he said after a while.

"I could make it a whole lot worse."

"What do you mean?"

"Look, you've got to put the past behind you and find something new."

"Now you sound like my mother, that's exactly what she says. 'You wouldn't have made a very good doctor anyway,' she goes on at me, 'you can't stand the sight of blood. Why don't you try law instead?' That's not the point! I'd feel a whole lot better about it if I'd been allowed to fail it myself. And that's precisely what I've set out to do."

Suzanne sighed.

"So you're happy to let them win?"

"All right! The bastards *have* won! They were always going to anyway, weren't they? After all, they had *their* chance when *they* were young to become what they are, and now they very conveniently forget that others need the same chance they were once given themselves."

"I've never seen you so angry before."

"It's there."

"No, Miles, it's because we're in this room. You've *got* to forget about it and put it behind you."

"Maybe. But it'll always be there, whatever happens."

"In that case," she said softly, reaching up to give him a gentle kiss, "we shall just have to do something about it, shan't we?"

Suzanne desperately wanted to help Miles all she could. She knew that his idle behaviour would have only one end and she decided that there was still time for him to alter his ways. They left the biology room in silence and headed back down the stairs to the ground floor.

"I've got double English for the first two periods," she said to him, "and then I've got nothing for the rest of the morning. Let's meet by your car at breaktime and go for a drive."

"Where shall we go?" asked Miles, a little surprised.

"I'll think of somewhere."

He watched her walk away and knew that this tall, beautiful blonde girl had touched his soul. He watched her until she was out of sight and then he made his way to the office to mark them both in the register. After that, he went up to the empty physics laboratory where he sat at the back of the room, reading through his physics textbook. It was an enormously large, heavy book that filled most of his briefcase and seemed to weigh a ton. He slowly thumbed his way through it from beginning to end, his mind in a state of confusion and turmoil. He didn't notice Mr Bates walking quietly through to the laboratory next door, but Mr Bates noticed him with mild surprise and approval. When the bell rang for break at half-past ten, he was still engrossed in his reading.

He sat up suddenly. "Oh!" he said to himself, realising the time, and got up quickly, putting the textbook back in his briefcase. He ran down to the yard at the back of the school where the car was parked behind the kitchens and Suzanne was already there. She was sitting on the front of the bonnet with her long legs stretched out luxuriously, one crossed over the other.

She prodded him with the toe of her right boot.

"Are you ready?"

Without waiting for him to reply, she drew one leg languorously back and swung herself around until her feet touched the ground. He opened the passenger door for her and she got in. He had left school by car many times in the past few months with Brian and Dave, usually to visit the pub, and thought nothing of it. But this was different. This had the feeling of a reckless escapade, the fulfilment of sexual longing. Miles sat in the driving seat. The warm smell of the leather interior, the fragrance of Suzanne's perfume and her own natural female scent went to his head, like some intoxicating cocktail that seemed to heighten his unspoken desire for her, and he knew that she shared that feeling. He turned the ignition key and the engine fired. Suzanne curled up beside him.

"Take me away from here," she murmured. "Take me where it's quiet and peaceful. Take me down by the river where we can hear only the sound of the water lapping past."

It was poetic and beguiling. Miles knew exactly the place that Suzanne had in mind and drove them there, leaving the town behind, following country roads and lanes until they arrived by the quietly-flowing river, meandering past fields and meadows. They parked the car by a gate and walked along the riverbank for some distance when eventually they reached a beautiful and secluded place where the river changed direction and herons waded. They sank down on to the long soft grass and Miles took her in his arms and kissed her. This time there were no interruptions because they lay alone together, far from anyone they knew or were ever likely to know. Unhurriedly they took their clothes off and pressed their bodies together, exploring each other. They were like two enraptured spirits lost to the world amidst the tall wavering grasses and ferns, with the sky above gazing down benevolently upon them, and nothing but the sound of distant birdsong, the flowing river and their ecstatic utterances. After they had finished making love, they lay dozing peacefully for a long time.

When she awoke, Suzanne lay on her back looking up at the sky, watching the clouds moving overhead.

"Miles," she said softly.

"Mmmmm?" he answered, stirring.

"Are you awake?"

"Yes."

"That was wonderful."

"I know."

"But do you know *why* it was wonderful? It was wonderful because it was the two of us out here in the middle of nowhere. Our love was as pure and simple as it could ever be. Perhaps this is what it was like for people in days gone by when they had nothing except each other – no possessions and no expectations. We expect too much of ourselves. Just imagine if we lived like this all the time."

"Are you saying that people in the past were happier?"

Suzanne rolled over and looked at him. "I don't know. How can we compare the different times we live in? All I'm saying to you is this: we take our lives much too seriously. You spoke to me earlier about your ambition and how it had been ruined. But does it really matter *that* much to you? Does it come before everything else?"

Miles looked deeply into her eyes.

"No," he said at last. "No, it doesn't. I have done something today that I never ever imagined I would do, or could do. I have fallen in love with the most adorable girl who ever existed and made love to her in a place that is so far removed from the world that I know – although in my heart I also know that this is how it *should* be. Our world is shallow but demanding. This world of ours, here, is wonderfully satisfying and yet undemanding. The heavens seem to be looking down on us, smiling. I feel more alive and happy today than I have ever done in my entire life and it is all because of you, dear Suzie, you have shown me something today that I hadn't realised."

"What is that?" asked Suzanne.

Miles put his hand between her legs and gently stroked her again.

"This," he said, "is the highest consideration of all."

Chapter 24

In the days that followed, Miles settled into a new routine of work, much to the surprise of Brian and the disbelief of Dave. There were occasional lapses from time to time. For instance, Miles knew that the most wonderful place in the entire school was the advanced chemistry laboratory, where the shelves were full of bottles containing chemicals and liquids in the most marvellous colours. He had a yearning to mix them all together in order to see what the result would be. A tincture of this and a drop of that, stirred over a bunsen flame, then add some of those lovely blue crystals, pour in a little of the red liquid and cut a thin slice of that curious roll of yellow metal kept in an oil-filled glass jar. It was far more exciting than the physics laboratory, where everything seemed so staid and prosaic. The chemistry laboratory, by contrast, was alive with possibilities, with the unexpected, with things that fumed, with violent reactions that exploded. He liked the faint whiff of chemicals that met him at the door when he entered the room, he liked the white starched lab coats and the eye-goggles, he liked the Periodic Table hanging on the wall, curling and cracked with age, he liked the taps and the washbasins set into the laboratory benches and he liked the gas-taps and the long lengths of rubber tubing. He was fascinated by pipettes and burettes, flasks and stoppers, stands and clamps, and imagined himself assembling an experiment that ran the whole length of the workbench. It was a room where things could *happen*. It seemed too risky and dangerous to be part of a school. Every time he stepped into the chemistry laboratory, he felt that he had entered a different world, a wondrous place where things fizzed, popped and banged.

One breaktime he proudly took Suzanne in to show her around. Brian and Dave were sitting at the back, grinning. The rest of the room was empty.

"That's where I sit, over there," he said, pointing to his lab stool.

Suzanne had given up chemistry after O-level and had never been in the advanced lab before.

"You must be very clever to know how it all works," she said, examining some of the apparatus that was already set up on the benches.

Miles smiled modestly.

"It's not that difficult when you get used to it," he said. "Of course, some experiments are harder than others. Would you like me to give you a demonstration?"

"It all looks rather dangerous to me," said Suzanne apprehensively. "Do you think you ought to?"

"Who's to know?" said Miles recklessly. "Now just sit down over there." He pointed to a stool in the corner. "Let's have a look at what we've got here." He ran an expert eye over the apparatus that somebody else had set up that morning and began fiddling about with various bottles and jars, taking liquids and powders from here and there and adding them to the concoction.

"Do you know what you're doing?" she asked nervously.

"I haven't got a clue," said Miles, giving her a cheerful smile. "But I've been wanting to do this for a long time." He lit a bunsen burner and placed it beneath a small stand that was supporting the flask into which he had poured the various liquids. He fastened a cork stopper into the top of the flask from which a thin glass tube protruded, leading to a condenser before heading off in the direction of more flasks and tubes. The mixture started bubbling at once and suddenly, without warning, it changed colour and whooshed through the tubes. Gaseous fumes began pouring out and the apparatus rocked alarmingly on the bench, as if it were coming to life. Finally there was a blinding flash from the beaker at the end and the apparatus collapsed in ruins.

"Miles!" screamed Suzanne, "What's happening?"

"Oh dear," said Miles, shaking his head sadly, "whatever will Mr Farley say when he gets back after break? Nothing ever usually goes wrong with Smith's experiments!"

They decided that it was time to leave the laboratory and took Suzanne for a long walk around the school before dropping her off at her next lesson when the bell rang for the end of breaktime. Then Miles, Brian and Dave slowly wandered back up to the lab, making sure that they were the last to arrive. When they got there, Smith was standing in the middle of the room, staring in dismay at his experiment while Mr Farley stood looking at him, waiting for an explanation.

"I don't understand it, sir," stammered Smith. "It was all right when I left it."

"Well it's not all right now," said Mr Farley in exasperation. "Clear up the mess at once and start again. And do it properly next time!"

"Yes, sir," mumbled Smith.

Miles strolled across to examine the blackened and twisted remains and shook his head sadly.

"Chemistry doesn't seem to be your best subject any more, does it, Smith? Firstly your poor lab coat and now this. What a shame."

But apart from that, Miles tried to turn himself into a hard-working sixth-former. Brian, in his idiotic fashion, did his best to keep up, and Dave merely despaired of them both and carried on with his somnific habits in the library, seeing himself as the new torch-bearer for all true layabouts. He did not feel abandoned or resentful in the way that he thought he might, for he still had Jane and his beer to think about, and after a while he even discovered that he too was going more often to lessons rather than be left entirely on his own.

Minus Davies tried to help Miles all he could.

"Work," he said encouragingly. "It's never too late."

"It already *is* too late," said Miles.

"No it isn't. The headmaster says he thinks you're going to do fine. He's got a lot of confidence in you."

Miles groaned.

"How *can* he have a lot of confidence in me when he doesn't even know who I am?"

Minus Davies wriggled uncomfortably in his chair.

"It's not my job to overrule the headmaster. If the headmaster says he's got a lot of confidence in you then that means the headmaster has got a lot of confidence in you – even if he doesn't know who you are."

Miles screeched and ran off. He decided to go to physics and start learning all his definitions. He got out his *Questions and Answers* textbook and stared at the problems and the diagrams until his eyes ached. He went to pure mathematics and grappled with Calculus and then he went to applied mathematics and wrestled with Statics and Dynamics. There was no end to it. Once he had solved one problem, there was another. He felt that his brain needed to have an infinite capacity to absorb it all. The only true respite came with the practical lessons. A physics practical lasted all morning and he enjoyed the conviviality of it, the silly seriousness of playing with springs and bouncing rubber balls, measuring the coefficient of restitution, connecting batteries to lamps and voltmeters and rheostats, examining the spectrum, listening to the Doppler Effect. They seemed like interesting children's party games, treated with great earnestness and seriousness of purpose.

Mr Bates enjoyed giving demonstrations. One day he sat beside the workbench, twiddling with the controls of the Van de Graaf electrostatic generator to produce static electricity. It was something that they had studied years earlier, but he took great pleasure in refreshing their memory with it. Everyone gathered dutifully behind him to watch while he plugged it into one of the wall sockets and switched it on. Slowly it began to make its low whirring sound, getting faster and faster until the magical sparks flashed between the large polished dome and the small metal ball which was fastened on the end of the long metal rod that stood next to it.

"Isn't it great?" said Mad Mike, pawing at Miles in excitement. Mr Bates turned the knob at the bottom to make it go even faster and it snapped away to itself while everyone stared in fascination.

Smith got close to it and peered at the elusive sparks through his thick spectacles.

"Be careful," warned Mr Bates.

"Why? Might it kill him?" asked someone hopefully. Smith turned around with a leer and snorted.

Mad Mike took Miles confidentially to one side.

"Have you come to join us at last?" he asked. "Have you seen what a good lot we are?"

Miles surveyed the class from where he stood, and then he turned to look back at the generator, now creating a vivid spark every second with the sound of a whiplash while everyone watched as though they had been hypnotised by it.

"Aren't we friends?" persisted Mad Mike. "Don't you realise how much I depend on you for advice?"

"Advice?" said Miles in puzzlement. "What advice?"

"You're a good friend," said Mad Mike. "You've done so much to help me."

"Oh, that's good," said Miles, not knowing why. "I'm so pleased."

Mad Mike did more to irritate Miles than anyone else, and that was probably why Miles got on with him so well. Mad Mike was desperately in love with Bobbie, who thought that Miles was a bad influence. Miles liked Bobbie very much and he didn't know why she thought he was a bad influence. What Mad Mike needed more than anything else *was* a bad influence to make him realise how much he depended on other people for help and advice. Thus having been badly advised, he would have to learn to make his own way in life. It was a crazy mixed-up world and Mad Mike didn't know whom he could trust, except himself. Sometimes he didn't even know if he could trust himself, and that made him feel even more despondent.

"My God!" he exclaimed one day, "I don't even know who can be trusted any more!"

"You can trust me," said Bobbie kindly, sidling up to him, and Mad Mike promised to trust her. "I won't tell anyone if you want to make love to me."

"You won't?" said Mad Mike, who wanted to very much but didn't know how to go about it.

"But I won't let *you* tell anyone, either," she insisted.

"I don't want to," said Mad Mike, and told Miles that he didn't want to tell anyone.

"Tell anyone what?" asked Miles, mystified.

"Oh, I can't tell you that," said Mad Mike, so Miles just guessed instead. Bobbie promised to keep her promise not to tell anyone that Mad Mike wanted to make love to her, which he did, and she kept her promise by not telling anyone. She didn't let him make love to her, either.

"Why not?" asked Mad Mike in disappointment. "Why won't you let me make love to you?"

"Because wanting isn't having," explained Bobbie, and Mad Mike felt that he had been dealt a crushing blow. He turned to Miles for help.

"She takes geology," he confided quietly, "and I think that's ever so lucky because they get to go on field-trips and things like that."

"What do they do when they go on field-trips?" asked Miles curiously.

"Oh, all sorts of things," said Mad Mike vaguely, gesticulating with his hands. "Look at rocks, I expect. Sometimes I wonder if I should have taken geology instead, because I would have been nearer to her then. It might have made it easier to get to university, too."

"Why do you want to go to university?" asked Miles. Mad Mike didn't know, he just had a horrible feeling inside him that he was done for and the thought used to send him into fits of passionate rage. While he stormed around the physics lab fretting, Smith pulled the plug of the electrostatic generator out from the wall as Mr Bates was preparing to switch it on again for another demonstration. A certain amount of confusion followed, and Mr Bates tried to pick up the generator at the same moment that Smith put the plug back in.

"Oh no," muttered Miles, "not *again*."

"Ouch!" yelled Mr Bates and collapsed on the floor.

"Is he dead?" asked someone, and Smith fainted.

Mr Bates wasn't really dead, he was simply being melodramatic, and he soon recovered his composure and got up off the floor. He sent Miss Starch into the small room at the back of the lab to make him a cup of tea. Smith was carried outside into the corridor and placed on the ground where he stayed with his eyes shut tight until everyone had gone back in and then he ran off home and got his mother to write a note saying he had been ill in bed all day with a high temperature.

Mr Bates was gently sipping his cup of tea when the deputy rushed into the room followed by the secretary, carrying a First Aid box.

"Who's dead?" demanded the deputy, searching all around the laboratory. "I can't see anyone who's dead, can you?"

"No," answered the secretary, and they paused to give each other a perceptive look.

"Nobody's dead," said Mr Bates. "Who said there was?"

"I heard there was an accident," replied the deputy. "I can't help it if there wasn't."

"I can't help it if there was," shrugged Mr Bates.

The deputy beckoned to the secretary and off they went again.

"A fine emergency that was," complained the secretary.

The deputy dragged her desperately to one side and told her all about the trouble he was having with his wife, who was middle-aged, stubborn and not very attractive.

"What I need is a fine woman like you," he yearned.

The secretary opened her eyes wide.

"Oh! I don't know what to say!" she said.

"Say you think I ought to leave my wife," said the deputy with all the cunning he could muster.

"I think you ought to leave your wife," said the secretary obligingly.

"Do you?" said the deputy in delight. "I think I will. I've needed a fine woman like you for years. My God, yes. Do you think I'll be able to get a divorce?"

"On what grounds?" asked the secretary, pursing her lips.

"Fornication?" hinted the deputy.

Apart from Miles, Brian and Dave, nothing changed whatsoever. Peter carried on drawing erotic pictures in the art room, Paul Brown carried on being captain of the school rugby team until the summer term when he became captain of the school cricket team, Francesca carried on typing letters all day in the school office and the headmaster carried on hiding in his study. The days of the examinations drew nearer and nearer, and all of their friends began revising. The atmosphere in the school became very serious.

Miles found himself in the headmaster's study where he wanted to tell them how much he was now working, but they wouldn't let him.

"Who are you?" queried the headmaster imperiously.

"This is the Peter I was telling you about, headmaster," explained the deputy.

"Sit down, Peter," offered the headmaster.

"I'm Miles, sir," said Miles helpfully. "I've come to tell you how hard I'm now working."

"Be quiet!" snapped the deputy. "This is the Peter who pretends he can draw disgustingly erotic pictures in the art room of young girls without any clothes on."

The headmaster opened his eyes in surprise.

"Really?" he murmured in disbelief. "Is he any good?"

"It's licentious and permissive!"

"Yes, of course it is!" said the headmaster, jerking himself up. He turned to Miles. "You ought to be ashamed of yourself, Peter!"

"I'm Miles, sir," sighed Miles.

"No you're not," corrected the headmaster, "you're Peter. Don't try and tell us our job, we know perfectly well who you are."

"I can prove who I am," said Miles.

"Prove who you're not," suggested the deputy with a superior inflexion in his voice.

"I don't play rugby, sir," said Miles, and the headmaster's face lit up.

"*I* know who you are!" he exclaimed suddenly, smacking his hand down on the desk. "You're Miles!" He turned triumphantly to the deputy. "This is Miles."

"Miles Randolph," said Miles, "from the second year sixth. I've come to tell you how hard I'm now working."

The deputy narrowed his eyes suspiciously.

"I thought it was," he declared with a frown.

"You may be wondering," said the headmaster at last, "how we discovered what you were doing with a certain young female member of the staff."

"No, sir," said Miles in surprise. "What certain young female member of the staff did you have in mind?"

The headmaster leaned forward and lowered his voice.

"Francesca."

Miles looked at them both in amazement.

"Did you say Francesca, sir?" he inquired.

"Yes," said the deputy bleakly, "he said Francesca. Don't pretend you haven't heard of her."

"I'm not pretending I haven't heard of her, sir."

"Are you sure you're not?"

"I'm sure I'm not."

"What exactly *were* you doing with her?" asked the headmaster slowly.

"But I thought you said you already knew what I was doing with her, sir. You asked me if I was *wondering* how you discovered what I was doing with her."

The headmaster cleared his throat.

"Oh, well I do, of course," he said hastily. "I only wanted

to hear it in your own words."

"I haven't been doing *anything* with her, sir," confessed Miles. "Whenever I'm late she marks me in the register, so I see her most days. That's all."

"Why are you late most days?" inquired the headmaster.

"If you really want to know, sir, it's because—" Miles stopped. Was there any point in going on? Did they really want to know the truth? Did they really want to know that he had fancied Francesca from the moment he first saw her, that he had felt sorry for her, that he had wanted to go to bed with her? Did they want to know that he had fancied any young lady teacher who went walking around the school in a ridiculously short mini-skirt and high-heeled shoes or, indeed, most of the girls in the sixth form? There was only one girl who meant anything to him now and that was Suzanne, but they didn't even know about her.

"Yes?" said the headmaster, leaning forward intently. "Because—?"

"It doesn't matter any more, sir," said Miles heavily. "I thought it did matter, I thought it mattered very much, but somehow I just don't think it matters at all."

And Miles forgot about everything that seemed to matter to him and when the time came he took his exams, and when he had finished taking them he emerged for the last time from the quietness of the examination hall, where Suzanne stood alone in the corridor waiting for him, and he laughed joyfully and threw all the precious question papers away before taking her in his arms and he didn't give a single damn what happened.